DIE FOR ME

A DI SCOTT BAKER CRIME THRILLER

JAY NADAL

INKUBATOR
BOOKS

Published by Inkubator Books
www.inkubatorbooks.com

ISBN (eBook): 978-1-83756-186-5
ISBN (Paperback): 978-1-83756-187-2
ISBN (Hardcover): 978-1-83756-188-9

Previously published by the author as Poison.

PROLOGUE

His eyes clamped shut as he clenched his teeth so tight, the muscles in his face stiffened and burnt. The memories. The pain. He thought he'd buried them deep, locked them away in a box with a thousand padlocks and chains, but he had been so wrong. It hadn't taken much, a simple trigger. An everyday event had invited the flashbacks in to haunt his fragile mind again.

He wasn't proud of it. That period of his life where he'd felt so weak, so feeble, so unable to stand up for himself. Humiliation had followed him. The smiles, the jeering, and jibes had left him broken.

But that was all behind him. Life was better, or so he'd believed.

He pulled away from his thoughts to stare out of the window. Behind the net curtain, he could stay inconspicuous and invisible. Tension rippled through his body. The tiny muscles around his eyelids flickered and twitched.

Deep breaths, deep breaths.

A soft melody played on his phone, an enchanting piece of music with a hypnotic effect. It calmed and soothed him.

Mary, Mary, quite contrary,
How does your garden grow?
With silver bells, and cockle shells,
And pretty maids all in a row.

He glanced at the clock. It would soon be time, and she would soon regret her actions.

Stood there in his jeans, he scrunched his bare toes into the carpet to ground himself. His eyes stared at life beyond the net curtains. He watched as an Asda delivery van pulled up, its driver then proceeding to unload several green crates onto his trolley before wheeling them into the doorway across the road.

A few yards away, a mother pushed her infant in a buggy. Her other child, a few years older, held onto the buggy with one hand, whilst stomping his feet and screaming loud enough to alert the whole street. His mother did little to calm him, occasionally yanking him by the back of his coat and bending down to shout in his ear, before giving him a whack across the back of his head.

He shook his head in frustration, itching to race across the road and slap the woman. She needed a taste of her own medicine. It was stupid bitches like her who spawned little oiks with no respect, discipline, or compassion.

A shiver raced down his spine as his fists tightened. He knew evil fighting evil achieved little, but sometimes it was the only way to get a person's attention. He ran his fingers over the ripples of skin on his stomach, arms, and chest. Tiny, rough folds of skin on a smooth background served as a constant reminder. His eyes squeezed shut as old memories flooded his mind.

Stop the thoughts, stop the thoughts. Get a fucking grip.

He checked the clock again. It had only felt like a few minutes, but he had been lost in his thoughts for over half an hour. With the music still playing in the background, he threw on a T-shirt, grabbed his coat, and left.

The crisp and cool air surrounded him as he stepped out onto the pavement. With the music still playing in his ears, he glanced up and down the street. She would be keen to see him. So naïve of her, but very soon she would regret ever setting eyes on him.

1

"What is the matter with people?" Ellen shouted, as traffic slowed to a crawl.

A lorry ahead of her attempted to overtake a bus dropping off passengers, only to find itself in a tight spot when a central crossing loomed into view. The lorry driver had no way of cutting into the gap between the central island and the bus. Car horns blared around her; drivers gesticulated with middle fingers, and mouthed expletives.

Ellen had thrashed out a routine with her daughter, Kitty, weeks ago. And so far it had worked out well, much to Kitty's annoyance at times. Her daughter hated being picked up every day from school, preferring instead to hang out with her mates. After all, that was what most of her friends did – it was what most kids of her age did. But Ellen, being overprotective, still believed she was too young to be roaming the streets. Even though Ellen had done so herself as a teenager, and it was something Kitty pointed out in every argument. Ellen would be quick to remind her how times had changed so much, and it wasn't as safe to do so any more.

Kitty had protested her independence during many heated conversations with her mum, often turning to her dad to back her up. Alan, not wishing to cross paths with his wife, would fold his arms, refusing to get involved, or conveniently remember he'd left something in the van.

After countless discussions, Kitty had agreed to being picked up each week on Monday, Wednesday, and Friday, giving her the other two days to hang out with her friends. But even this small glimmer of freedom carried caveats. She was to be home no later than five p.m. or she would be grounded for a week, with no access to her phone at the weekend.

At first, Kitty had grumbled and stomped around the house in a foul mood before realising some freedom was better than nothing. And she had shuddered at the prospect of losing her mobile phone at the weekends and being unable to talk to her friends. It was clear in her mind that her parents didn't realise the importance of a mobile phone. It was a teenager's lifeline, their only access to a wide world beyond the confines of their pokey bedrooms. They could sit there for hours looking at TikTok videos, liking people's Instagram pictures, and video calling one another to swap and practise beauty tips, or talk about which boys were peng or dank. Ellen had never heard of such references and soon discovered they meant attractiveness in teen circles.

Ellen tapped her fingers on the steering wheel as she waited for the congestion to clear. She hit the redial button on her steering wheel and waited for her phone to connect. It dialled Kitty's number, reaching her voicemail yet again.

Kitty's recorded message pumped through the speakers

in the car. "Hi, this is Kitty. I'm not around, so tough..." Her daughter then erupted into fits of laughter. It was a message she'd recorded whilst sitting with friends, and they had all thought it was hilarious.

Ellen tutted. "Kitty, love, it's me. I'll be with you in a few minutes. I'm stuck in bloody traffic. Typical. Call me as soon as you get this message. Love you lots."

She disconnected her third call. Yes, Kitty was lazy about answering her phone, especially when it was one of her parents, but by now she must have realised her mum needed to talk to her. The traffic ahead of Ellen cleared, as the lorry gave way to the bus before it slipped in behind it. She accelerated away, still furiously tapping on the steering wheel, as if that was going to make her miraculously appear at the pickup point.

The corner of St Helens Park had been agreed as the place Ellen would pick up Kitty. As she pulled up next to the kerb, she glanced around for her daughter. Confused, Ellen looked over her shoulder in case Kitty was behind her. There was no sign of her. Her eyes scanned the park next. Maybe she was walking around with a friend, but on a cold winter's afternoon, Ellen could see the park was deserted.

She stepped out from her car and walked around to the pavement. She continued to scan her surroundings. Every movement attracted her scrutiny.

Kitty was nowhere to be seen.

Ellen reached into her coat pocket and pulled out her phone, hoping Kitty might have left a text message. Nothing. She pressed redial and waited for her call to connect. Ellen tapped her foot impatiently as Kitty's voicemail message played again.

"Kitty sweetheart, it's Mum again. Did you forget I'm

picking you up today? Where are you? Call me back."

Ellen sighed. Kitty was usually here as agreed most of the time. On the odd occasion she forgot, she would shrug her shoulders dismissively while her mum told her off. The fact that Kitty never returned her phone calls only infuriated Ellen further. Ellen had explained to Kitty about the importance of replying. It didn't matter how concerned she was for her daughter's safety; her pleas would go in one ear and out the other.

Concern and panic gripped Ellen, making her skin tingle. She wrapped her arms around her chest to keep the cold out as she marched back to the car.

The journey home took ten minutes. Ellen slammed the car door, locking it with her key fob as she rushed towards her front door. Once in, she dropped her bag by the bottom of the stairs and dashed into the kitchen. She would often find the evidence from a scavenger hunt for food. A half-empty Coke can would be sitting on the kitchen work surface, the empty wrapper from a cheese string would have been discarded where it had been eaten, and the lid from the biscuit barrel would be open, allowing the biscuits to go stale.

But the kitchen was as she'd left it that morning – spotless.

Her eyes narrowed in confusion and her brow creased. There was no sign of her daughter in the lounge either. The TV would often be left on after Kitty had flicked through the channels, decided there was nothing on, and gone to her bedroom.

Ellen climbed the stairs.

"Kitty? Are you home?"

She felt foolish as the words left her mouth, because

Kitty's shoes and bag weren't behind the door where she normally left them. She opened the door to her daughter's bedroom, finding it just as it had been left that morning. Her bed was unmade, clothes were strewn across the floor, and her curtains were still drawn. She was like any teenager, impossible to stir in the mornings and even harder to talk to during the first thirty minutes after she woke, offering nothing more than a grunt or groan in response to any questions Ellen would ask.

When Kitty came down the stairs each morning, Ellen would greet her with, "Morning darling, can I get you breakfast?"

Kitty would respond with a scowl, and a look of hatred that suggested, "You spoilt my sleep. I hate you. Stay out of my space."

At this precise moment of not knowing where her daughter was, Ellen would have gladly welcomed a death stare. Her worry intensified. Thoughts tumbled through her mind. The walk from the school to their meeting place was no more than a ten-minute stroll, fifteen minutes if she really dawdled.

Something didn't feel right, and if Kitty was playing games, or being absent-minded, God help her when she returned.

Ellen stood by her front window, looking out across the garden and the road. Her eyes darted from left to right, searching for any sign of her daughter approaching. She wondered where she could be. Perhaps she was with one of her friends. Ellen got the impression she had way too many friends and often wondered how many were real and how many were ones she'd never met. She knew Kitty hung around with one of them often: Claudia White.

Scrolling through her contact list on her phone, Ellen pulled up the number for Emma White, Claudia's mum, and dialled it.

"Hi, Emma, it's Ellen here, Kitty's mum. Is Kitty with you?"

"Sorry, Ellen, no she isn't. Has she not come home?"

"No, I was due to pick her up, but she didn't show. I came home thinking she may have forgotten, but Kitty's not here. I thought Claudia may have been with her or seen her?"

"I doubt it, Ellen. I picked up Claudia from the school gates today. It's our weekly food shop day, so I always drag Claudia with me."

"Can you ask her if she saw Kitty at the end of school?" Ellen asked.

"Sure, hang on a sec."

There was a muffled exchange in the background before Emma White came back on the line. "Sorry, Ellen, Claudia was at the other end of the school for her last lesson, so she would have come out a different gate to Kitty."

"Okay. Thanks, Emma. If Claudia thinks of anything, can you let me know?"

"Of course. I'm sure she'll turn up looking all sheepish before you know it." Emma's attempt at injecting light humour into the conversation didn't lessen her worry.

Ellen called the school next, only to find out there were no after-school activities today and the school gates were closed at four p.m., after the last pupils had left. The only staff left on site were the school secretary, the caretaker, and two cleaners.

Torn between staying put and searching for Kitty, Ellen bit her bottom lip and argued with her herself. She couldn't sit here while Kitty was out there somewhere, hopefully safe, but out there. And with the winter darkness setting in for the afternoon, Ellen raced from the house and jumped back in her car. The roads in the dark took on a menacing feel. The trees lining the streets were nothing more than skeletal puppets that swayed in the gentle breeze, their branches bending towards her, as if pointing their suspicion at her.

Her eyes scanned the pavements, her car crawling slower than a learner driver on their first terrifying lesson. Beginning from the school gates, Ellen worked her way along the route Kitty would have taken if she'd walked home. In the darkness, figures were harder to make out. Their shadows moved, but their faces were obscured.

Ellen pulled up to the kerb and stepped out of her car when she saw a large crowd of schoolkids ahead of her. She recalled Kitty telling her that she'd hang around here often. With a chip shop and games store close by it was a hub, a gathering place for all the local kids. The noise of laughter, of girls screaming, and boys chanting grew louder as she got nearer.

Circling the crowd, Ellen scanned the faces. Her eyes tracked from one child to the next. She stopped and asked each group of girls. Her questions about Kitty was met with sniggers and shaking heads.

Kitty wasn't there.

She returned home.

Two hours had passed since Kitty had gone missing. No one had seen or heard from her. Ellen paced back and forth across her lounge, stopping every few minutes to check her phone and peek through the blinds.

Out of her mind and gripped with panic, Ellen made two calls, one to her husband, the other to the police.

2

An explosion in her brain sent her world spinning in circles... the type that carried more possibilities than she could be conscious of... but dozens of ideas swirled there in that buzz of electricity racing through her body... she could feel it. It was the calling card of adventure, excitement and dares, and of paths opening up in front of her.

She smiled a warm, smug smile that reddened her cheeks, while her eyes bobbed around in their sockets. She wanted to climb a mountain and fly through the air effortlessly, like seagulls gliding over the sea. It all seemed possible now, nothing could stop her. Whatever lay ahead would be a wonderful challenge, and there might be tears, but it was her adventure to take, and so she smiled wider. The ideas would come, probably when she least expected it. She tipped her head back and let her imagination dance carefree.

Kitty felt giddy with excitement. She wanted to run, to shout, to tell everyone what was going to happen... but she waited. She felt pumped, excited, more alive than she had ever thought possible. She couldn't sit still because her legs trembled so much; she couldn't stand because she kept swaying; she couldn't utter a single word through her numb lips. Her mind was like a butterfly. Whatever distraction she chose for herself, it kept fluttering back to the words being spoken to her and the hand holding hers.

"Not long now, and then you'll be free to soar high like the birds."

Then she'd get that tingly feeling all over again.

As each hour passed, her mind swayed back and forth with greater intensity. It felt like she was bouncing off the walls. Sweat beaded on her face. Her clothes clung to her soft, tender, milky-white skin. Every fibre of her being vibrated with anticipation, as adrenaline coursed through her veins. Her hands trembled and her eyes were fixed in a wide stare at the ceiling. There was no worrying about the past and no anxiety about the future.

This was her time.

3

___

Scott heard panting behind him. He slowed his pace so Cara could catch up.

In recent weeks he had managed to convince her to join him for his morning run along the seafront, even though Cara preferred to avoid exercise at all costs. Scott sounded like a broken record whenever he drilled into her the importance of keeping up her cardiovascular levels because of her less physical job. That last reference had sparked several heated conversations between them as she'd gone to great lengths to explain how she didn't just sit on her arse all day.

They'd reached a mutual truce after agreeing it was the right thing to do.

Cara loved winding Scott up. She loved Scott's energetic and vibrant approach to health and wellbeing. She had even tried to convince Scott of joining him in a few months as a fair-weather runner, but Scott had argued there was no better time than now to brush off the winter blues, and lose the few extra pounds gained over Christmas.

Running on a cold winter's morning wasn't her idea of fun, especially after last night. They had attended a birthday dinner for her cousin, Charlotte, one of the few occasions where Scott had met her family. They had met in a small restaurant in The Lanes and being a Monday night, it hadn't been too busy.

They had laughed during the evening after Cara's batty aunt had not only drunk too much but badgered Scott and Cara about their future plans. The topic of marriage had surfaced more than a few times over the course of the evening, as had the expectation of children on the horizon, and if so, how many, and did they have a preference between boys and girls.

Scott and Cara had done a sterling job in batting off and deflecting most of her questions by focusing on how lovely the food was and topping up her wine glass. But Cara's aunt was far too shrewd for their young tomfoolery and had continued to press home her points about not leaving it too late, and that Cara's biological clock was ticking away. It had led to a mixture of amusing and embarrassing exchanges between Scott and Cara.

Cara had felt awkward at her aunt's inquisition, and knew Scott had felt the same. It was something people would speculate about the longer they stayed together, but their future wasn't something they brought up. Cara often avoided bringing up the subject, even though she wanted children. She knew Scott would be a wonderful father, but in her heart, she knew Scott didn't want any more children after losing his family.

If they had a little girl, would Scott always be comparing her to his first daughter, Becky? Cara knew she was being stupid for even entertaining the thoughts, but they nevertheless lingered in the back of her mind. Whenever she thought about having children over the years, she'd imagined having one of each. Ideally starting with a boy, so he could look after his little sister.

Her aunt had been right, her biological clock was ticking, but a part of her felt too scared to open up to Scott.

"Come on, babes, not far to go, and then we can turn around," Scott shouted over his shoulder.

Cara huffed and puffed, her run slowly descending into a fast walk, as a wintry chill bit into her cheeks and left her with a red glow. Unable to run any farther, she pulled up and leant against the railings overlooking the beach, to catch her breath. Scott was a few yards ahead of her before he realised Cara had stopped. He continued his run in a small circle before backtracking to Cara.

"You can't stop now. It's this last bit when you push yourself through the barriers that make all the difference. Trust me, you will feel fantastic afterwards."

Cara shot him a disparaging look. "Trust... me, *you* won't be feeling... fantastic when I kick you in the nuts... for making me do this," she said through gasps of air. Her chest heaved as she tried to flood her body with oxygen.

Scott rolled his eyes and continued to jog on the spot, like an overenthusiastic personal trainer geeing along his fat-loss clients in a condescending way.

Cara shook her head and waved her hands in surrender. "I'm done. I can't go any farther. You can carry on, but I'm going to turn around and *walk* back."

Scott stopped and rested his hands on his hips. "That's a cop-out. I promise, it gets much easier the more you do it. You'll feel more energetic, you'll feel alive, and you'll have a buzz for the rest of the day."

Cara looked around her, looking for anything to throw at Scott. "Scottie, I'm doing this at my own pace. I've come farther today than I have so far, so that's progress. Hopefully, when I come out for a run next time, I'll be able to go a little farther. Don't forget, I'm not as fit as you."

Scott moved in closer and wrapped his arms around her waist. "From where I'm looking, you're more than fit." He kissed her softly on her forehead.

Cara looked up at him with a mischievous glint in her eyes. "How about we both go home? I promise you, I can get your heart rate up in different ways and you'll burn just as many calories, and it will be so much more fun..."

The corner of her mouth curled up in a smile.

Scott looked up at the sky before levelling his eyes with her and shaking his head. "You're unbelievable."

Cara shrugged a shoulder. "I know... Well?"

"I'll race you back, last one in bed has to have a cold shower," Scott shouted as he raced off.

Cara smiled to herself. *It works every time.*

HER BODY FELT EUPHORIC, her skin was tingling, prickly, like a thousand needles were poking her. She couldn't remember if she'd slept much last night, as her mind drifted in and out of reality. She remembered words, a hand stroking her face, a cool liquid being offered to her lips, but that was it. Now all she could hear was the hum of traffic, engines being revved, noises fading in and out of her awareness.

Kitty smiled. *This feels so good.*

She danced on the spot, her arms outstretched, as she pirouetted on the spot and stared up at the sky. One minute her heart was hammering in her chest, the next it had calmed into a hypnotic beat. The lights flashed around her, creating sparkling explosions of coloured brilliance that blinded her. She closed her eyes and watched the light show play out on the back of her eyelids.

Kitty inched closer to the edge, her eyes widening as she stared at everyday life being played out beneath her. From up here, people looked like little ants scurrying along the pavements. Cars nudged other cars along the road, crawling bumper-to-bumper. She was ready to leap into the sunshine with nothing but air beneath her feet.

And then she was gone, eyes wide, her smile even wider.

4

Having enjoyed his second shower in the space of an hour, Scott sat on the side of the bed with a towel draped across his lap. He still had a bit of time before he needed to be at work for the afternoon. Cara lay beside him, the duvet partially covering her body, one large and round breast fully exposed. She didn't take her eyes off Scott as he ran his fingers through his wet hair. He tried to avoid looking too long at her, even as she ran her fingers up and down his back, a sure sign Cara wanted more of him.

It would be all too easy to jump back in bed and wrap his arms around her, feasting on her sexuality. He knew that once she kissed his neck, his resistance would crumble. After a few delicate touches of her warm lips, his hands would start to do her bidding and it would be game over. She carried an Amazonian appeal he doubted any man could ignore. A natural magnetism which drew men to her, and fortunately for him, he was the lucky one.

He struggled to pretend it didn't bother him, but seduction was what Cara did best whenever she moved closer, giving him just the right, heated look. She didn't just look at him; she looked into him, as if knowing his deepest desires. It happened every time. With the kiss came the smooth touch of her body, with the right blend of confidence and sexual tension. It had always been that way between them. Whenever they gazed at each other, the chemistry grew and a stronger seed of love was planted, followed by an open invitation to learn more about one another, and a chance for their bodies to communicate without the need for words.

Scott's phone lit up on the bedside table, and he glanced at it. It was a text message from Abby, telling him to contact her at once. He was about to reach over when Cara grabbed it first.

"Please... give me one more hour. Abby is back at the office, and she is more than capable of handling anything. Please?" Her eyes were longing as she arched her back, inviting Scott to join her.

"Will you behave? She said 'at once' it must be serious." Scott wrestled the phone from her, leaving Cara to roll over and grumble her dissatisfaction.

Scott dialled Abby's number and waited for her to pick up. "Hi, Abby, is everything okay?"

"I'm not disturbing you am I, guv?" Abby asked.

Scott smiled at a sulking Cara. "No. I was getting ready to head into the office. What's up?"

"A young girl went missing yesterday afternoon and has died in suspicious circumstances."

A YOUNG GIRL.

Abby's words haunted him as Scott made his way towards the scene. His lips thinned into a grimace when he got stuck in a long line of traffic that snaked along Preston Road, with a tailback all the way to Preston Park. Despite having an afternoon off, Cara sat in the passenger seat, her medical bag with her at all times in case of an emergency call-out like this one.

Scott pulled up behind a paramedic fast-response car parked inside the outer-cordon tape. Scott and Cara signed in on the scene log before making their way towards the inner cordon. Neither of them ever wanted to witness a scene like this first hand. Grim-faced police officers stood guard, keeping onlookers at a safe distance. Other officers stood in small huddles, discussing their own thoughts, theories, and feelings. Many uniformed officers had become hardened to scenes such as these, often being the first ones to arrive. But the death of a child always added an extra layer of anxiety and grief, which most officers found hard to cope with.

Traffic came to a standstill in both directions. Shops lined one side of the street, with small residential dwellings above. On the opposite side was a uniform row of Victorian terraced housing, with splendid architectural features, each one sporting a basement apartment. It was an area of town popular with students from the university. There were plenty of student pubs and fast-food takeaways to serve them. Guitar shops sat next to kebab shops, small food stores, and vegan cafés. It was an eclectic mix that added vibrancy and cultural depth to Brighton.

Scott looked up at the viaduct. A red-and-brown brick railway bridge adorned the top, built in the mid-eighteen hundreds, with dressings of yellow brick and stone. The structure was a historical part of Brighton's transition through the ages. The grade-two-listed structure consisted of an elliptical arch fifty feet wide over Preston Road, and twenty-six round arches thirty feet wide along its length. At nearly seventy feet high, it was an imposing structure and an integral feature of the Brighton landscape. From where Scott stood, it looked taller.

A nearby officer handed Scott a pack of white overalls and blue booties, whilst Cara extracted her own from her work case. Abby, having noticed Scott's arrival, made her way towards him. With a sombre and serious look on her face, she ripped off her face mask. Beyond her and in the distance, a blue tarpaulin had been erected by fire fighters, shielding onlookers from the worst of it. SOCO had positioned their white tent to cover the remains.

"What have we got, Abby?" Scott asked, pulling up the zip of his white suit.

Abby blew out her cheeks. "We believe it's the remains of fourteen-year-old Kitty Morris, who went missing on her way home from Causeway secondary school in Hove. Witnesses saw her fall from the top of the viaduct."

"Oh my God," Scott gasped, as his eyes travelled back up to the top of the viaduct.

"I nearly threw up. It's a fucking mess behind there." Abby exhaled, shaking her head in disbelief, and staring at the ground. She took a swig of water.

"What do we know about her?"

"Her mum was supposed to pick her up yesterday, but Kitty didn't turn up at the agreed pickup point. Her mum spent the next two hours looking for her before calling the police. A MisPer report was logged, and officers began searching for her last night when they realised it wasn't a prank."

"And can we be sure it's her?" Scott asked.

Abby nodded. "Evidence recovered from the scene seems to confirm her identity, including her schoolbag and mobile phone. Both matched the description given by her mum."

"Was anyone else seen up there?" Scott asked, as he looked up at the viaduct, his eyes following the path of the decorative brick topping.

Abby shook her head to confirm eyewitnesses didn't remember seeing anyone else. "Most of them admitted they'd been frozen to the spot when they saw Kitty fall. A couple of them mentioned the loud thud and crack, followed by what people described as a wet sound."

"The kind of sound a large watermelon would make if it was dropped from a height onto a hard surface." Scott pushed away images of the impact and the damage left from his mind.

"Do you think it was a prank or suicide?" Cara asked, as she picked up her bag.

Scott shrugged. "That's what we'll have to find out."

Cara headed off to join her colleagues in forensics who were examining the body.

"We are waiting for British Transport Police to give us clearance to get up there," Abby added. " It's a live line, so they won't let any of our officers up there. And because the line is under their jurisdiction, the BTP want to be the first to examine the scene."

The thought of viewing the body made Scott's intestines twist, as he made his way towards the forensic tent. He paused outside, taking in a deep breath, before he lifted one flap and peered inside. Bile raced up his throat, a scorching heat that left bitterness in his mouth. Beads of sweat peppered his forehead as his eyes scanned the scene. Abby had been right. It was carnage.

There was little left of the girl's head. She was a child. In her school uniform, she looked even younger, slender arms and legs contorted in different directions. He noticed the fingers on both hands were splayed out as if she'd been trying to cushion her fall. Her grey skirt clung tightly to her upper thighs. The white swoosh on her black Nike trainers had been coloured in with a blue felt-tip pen, and her once-white school shirt beneath a black blazer was now a patchwork of crimson red shades. Her eyes stared off into the distance, displaying their own shock at what she had done. The back of her head did indeed resemble a crushed watermelon, with remnants of her brain and bone fragments splattered in an arc around her. She was on her back, with her head twisted to one side. Scott knew the impact would have been instant death.

Scott stepped away from the tent, leaving Cara to do her work. She shot him a quick glance before he left. There was anguish and sadness in her eyes. Scott took a few moments outside the tent to gather his thoughts and contain his emotions. He had seen victims in a similar state before but never a child.

Matt Allen, the crime scene manager, joined Scott a few moments later to discuss the evidence taking process. Abby headed off to oversee the work of her uniformed colleagues, to make sure they captured the details and statements of the eyewitnesses before checking for any CCTV footage.

The increased police presence and traffic delays had an immediate effect on the town. Frustrated drivers, unaware of the tragedy ahead, did U-turns to find another way to reach their destinations. Small crowds gathered, whispering behind hands, thrashing out their own theories, pointing fingers and shaking their heads.

In the middle of his discussion with Matt, Scott paused for a moment to watch one of Matt's colleagues carry a clear evidence bag away from the scene, its contents obvious to the naked eye. They were Kitty's personal possessions. A pink Nike rucksack was covered in marker pen doodles, names and heart shapes. The rucksack reflected the fun and carefree adolescent life Kitty had once enjoyed. The poignancy wasn't lost on Scott as it drove home the significance of what he was dealing with.

"I need you to make this a number-one priority for you and your team, Matt. This is not only tragic but bloody horrific. I have no idea what I'm going to tell her parents." Scott sighed.

"I'll make sure of that. I've got the easier job and I feel for you. Her parents are going to want answers."

"I know. And I haven't got any for them."

5

"Okay, team," Scott began with a soft tone, "It's been a tough day and we are all hurting, but we need to think this through with clear heads, even if we have heavy hearts." He wheeled the whiteboard around to face his team and wrote Kitty Morris's name in the middle with a question mark beside it. He pinned up a picture taken from the scene at the viaduct.

As he stared at the innocent victim, his mind drifted back to the horrific scene. Whilst investigations had continued, they'd sealed off the surrounding area. Even with darkness creeping in, forensic investigators had continued their fingertip search of the scene with uniformed colleagues. Flashes of brilliance had lit up the ground as SOCOs photographed the area in detail; arc lights had allowed their work to continue, uninterrupted.

As the evening rush hour added further congestion to the area, diversions had been put in place to steer traffic away from the area. All available officers had been pulled in to help with the huge traffic chaos that had ensued. With

Brighton's narrow and twisting streets, slow-moving traffic and congestion was a part of daily life. But an incident on this scale had led to much of Brighton coming to a standstill, while one of the major routes in and out of Brighton remained closed.

With Meadows being away at a conference, Scott had left him a message saying he would update him when he returned to the office tomorrow.

"We are working on the assumption the deceased is Kitty Morris. At six p.m. yesterday evening, Kitty was reported as missing by her mum, Ellen Morris. A risk assessment was carried out, and Kitty's disappearance was considered a high risk because it was out of character for her. Uniformed officers began with a detailed search of the area around Causeway secondary school in Hove where she was a pupil."

Scott stood beside the whiteboard. An uncomfortable silence hung in the air; the usual light-heartedness at the team briefings was replaced by a dark and sombre mood, reflected back in the faces of his officers. His words were met with silence and a few nods.

"Any sightings of her?" Raj asked, sipping on a mug of tea, which he cupped between his hands.

Scott shook his head. "Nothing. Officers extended their search along the possible route Kitty would have taken if she had walked home. She was due to meet her mother on Hangleton Way by St Helens Park, as agreed."

"What did her mum do?" Raj continued.

"According to her mother, Kitty was always there within ten minutes of finishing school. When her mum turned up and found no sign of her, she checked the park, then retraced Kitty's route, visiting all the places where she might hang out. But no one had seen anything."

"No answer from her phone?"

"Ellen left several messages for Kitty, but none of them were returned." Scott pinned up a detailed aerial view of Hove and circled the pickup point. He then drew another circle around Kitty's school and tapped the spot. "As you can see, there is only one road Kitty would have taken from her school to where she would have met her mum. It's primarily a residential area, and there would have been a lot of kids travelling in the same direction as her."

"So, she just vanished, guv?" Mike speculated, as he tapped a finger on his chin.

"On the face of it, yes. Kitty's mum called one or two of her friends, and she also contacted the school in case Kitty had been held back in detention or at an after-school activity that she wasn't aware of. According to the school, the gates were closed at four p.m."

"Her mum must've been beside herself,' Mike said. 'It's cold, it gets dark early, so it makes searching even harder. Poor cow."

Even though his intentions were sincere, Mike's choice of words always bordered on being a little crass.

Scott continued. "With her body only having been discovered this afternoon, we need to know what happened to her in the preceding twenty-four hours. What were her last known movements?"

Abby chipped in. "We have access to her phone, so we can download her GPS coordinates, as well as any recent conversations."

Scott agreed and suggested they needed to look at anyone she'd had contacted within the last twenty-four to thirty-six hours. He tasked Helen with looking into Kitty's social media profile, to which Abby suggested she start with

Instagram, Snapchat and TikTok, making a reference to her own kids.

"One thing I've noticed from seeing how my two rely on social media so much is how they practically live out their lives on those bloody sites. Dance tutorials, hairstyling tips, swapping in and out of clothes, pranks, dares, sharing sad stories... The list goes on. It's like nothing is private any more. The social media sites turn a spotlight on every nook and cranny of your life. I hate it when the kids try to get me involved in it." Abby shuddered as she recalled recent examples, one being the lyric challenge her daughter Sophie had tried to rope her into, with disastrous results. Abby hated anything to do with singing and knew she sounded like a strangled cat, so for Sophie to stitch her up with a challenge that, unbeknown to her, Sophie had posted to all her friends, ranked up there as one of those points in life where she wanted to crawl under a stone.

"Start with her profiles. Who was she talking to, what posts was she liking, were there any recent friend requests etc.?" Abby said.

Scott jotted these points down on the whiteboard as a reminder. He added, "The twenty-four-hour period between approximately three thirty p.m. yesterday and three p.m. today are crucial to our investigation. Where was she? Was she hiding out somewhere? Or was someone covering for her?"

"I often find friends know a lot more than they let on," Abby surmised. "Kids keep secrets between themselves and then swear blindly they know nothing. I definitely think it's worth talking to her friends again. They may be scared to open up to begin with, but they may be able to give us an insight into her whereabouts in the last twenty-four hours."

Scott agreed, and asked Abby to follow through with that. He instructed the team to get officers to start doing door-to-door enquiries nearer the school, and on the route she would have taken along Hangleton Way before meeting her mum.

"Make sure officers pay particular attention to any properties with CCTV footage that may have recorded the last twenty-four to forty-eight hours. We want all copies back here for analysis," Scott insisted.

Mike leant back in his chair and folded his arms. He rested them on his pot belly which served as a convenient shelf. "You think it was a prank that went wrong, or suicide? I mean, you'd have to be in a pretty fucked up place to want to take your life in that way. And if it was a prank, then you'd have to have the bollocks to go up there. Maybe things went horribly wrong."

Scott shifted from one foot to another and stuffed his hands in his pockets. "At the moment, I think we need to keep an open mind. We don't know anything about Kitty or her mental state. If it was suicide, then we need to understand what was going on in her life that made her feel she needed to end it."

"And if it was a prank?" Mike speculated, raising a brow.

"Then we need to find out who else was involved. Perhaps you're right. Maybe it was a prank that went horribly wrong. We also need to understand how she got up there in the first place. It's a railway bridge, with a live line, seventy feet up in the air. That's one spectacular dare." Scott turned and stared at the picture of the viaduct on the whiteboard.

"What could Cara tell us from her initial examination?" Helen asked.

Scott grimaced. "There wasn't much left of our victim. The body needs to be cleaned up at the mortuary for Cara to do a more detailed investigation. The post-mortem is scheduled to take place tomorrow once Kitty's identity has been confirmed by her parents. But the poor girl was a real mess; it's going to take a bloody miracle to tidy her up enough for her parents to identify her."

Helen asked if the parents knew, to which Scott confirmed they had been informed of a tragic incident this afternoon involving a girl of school age and to prepare for the worst. He added a family liaison officer was with them at the moment.

"Right, team, you need to go home and get some sleep, because we are going to be busy tomorrow. Helen and I are going to visit the parents now, which is something I'm not looking forward to."

6

Scott pulled the collar up on his coat as he exited the car and searched for the address. The sound of Helen's low heels clicking on the pavement broke the silence of the night. The soft-yellow glow from street lights bounced off roofs of parked cars as they made their way towards the house. On first sight, the street seemed pleasant enough, a smart, suburban tree-lined avenue with semi-detached houses, clean frontages, and well-maintained gardens.

Even though Abby had agreed to stay on in her job, Scott was still mindful of her indecisiveness about it. Scott had come up with a solution with Helen, allowing Abby to be home with her kids. Even though it was working, he worried about Abby's final comments as the briefing ended. She'd felt numb and paralysed after seeing the body. Scott understood her reaction. He'd felt the same upon seeing the remains. No matter how hard officers tried to leave emotions out of it, it was impossible. Many colleagues had their own children, like Abby, which only made tragedies like this more real.

It was a feeling he knew too well, and not a day passed without him thinking of his own daughter, Becky, who would have been nine now. He'd spent many an hour imagining what Becky would have been like. All those missed opportunities he would never get a chance to experience, like her school nativity plays at Christmas, watching her at the school sports day, or even opening her presents on her birthday. Simple pleasures that many parents took for granted would have been the most precious moments to him, on reflection. Becky had been into everything, and no doubt she would have been enjoying the last few years of primary school, where life was so pure and innocent. He had no doubt she would have been cheeky, in the same way her mum was. He smiled when he thought of the times Tina and Becky used to gang up on him, and he would have happily paid that price again to still have them here.

Scott paused by the front gate and looked at a clean, white-fronted property, with a trendy, black-composite door. The garden was decorated in loose black slate, with an ornate tree in the middle. A navy MINI Clubman belonging to Andrea Smith, the FLO, was parked outside on the street. He hated this bit more than anything else and took a deep breath before ringing the doorbell.

Andrea answered and gave Scott a slight nod.

"How are they doing?" Scott whispered.

Andrea shrugged. "Not good. The mum is in bits, under-standably. They took the dad to the mortuary, despite being advised not to until the body was tidied up. He was starting to lose it a bit and insisted he'd rather get it over and done with and know sooner than later. The mortuary team did a quick rush job of preparing the body. We'll know any minute."

"Did she identify Kitty's rucksack and phone?"

Andrea nodded. "That's when she proper lost it. Crumpled to the floor in a heap."

Scott followed Andrea through to the lounge where she introduced him to Kitty's mum. Ellen Morris remained seated, her hands clutching a bunch of tissues in her lap. She had long, dark hair pulled into a ponytail; her round face was streaked with tears. Ellen wore a thick cable-knit jumper and tight jeans, with fluffy slippers. She appeared to shiver occasionally, which Scott imagined was more through shock than anything else.

"Mrs Morris, I'm Detective Inspector Scott Baker, and this is Detective Constable Helen Swift. I'm the senior investigating officer in this case, and we believe the child involved in this tragic incident this afternoon is your daughter, Kitty. Unfortunately, for formal reasons, we still needed the body to be identified, which I understand your husband has been taken to the mortuary to do that."

Ellen stared at Scott through puffy, red eyes, her cheeks peppered with red.

"I know it's a difficult time for you but I do need to ask you a few more questions, if that's okay?"

Ellen nodded as Scott and Helen dropped onto the sofa opposite her. Helen got out her notepad and pen, to take down any points of interest.

"Do you think anything was bothering Kitty?" Scott began.

"No. Everything was normal. She went to school in the morning and I said goodbye to her. And... now she's not here," Ellen replied, her voice monotone and raspy.

"What kind of girl was she?"

Ellen shrugged. "Like any other girl her age. Into music, fashion... She hated doing homework, she lived on take-aways, and hated my home cooking..." Ellen trailed off as a small smile broke on her face. Then she began to cry.

Scott continued to ask a few questions, but made little headway with Ellen, as she swapped between bouts of crying and anger.

"The police should have found her! Twenty-four hours. She was missing for twenty-four hours. How could a four-teen year old not be found for that long?" Ellen shouted, directing her anger and frustration at Scott. She thumped her thighs.

"Mrs Morris, I can assure you our officers did everything possible to locate your daughter. What we need to do now is find out what happened."

The wailing began anew, raw emotions seeping from every pore, as Ellen dropped her head into her hands. Scott glanced at Helen who, going by her reddened eyes, was visibly moved. Scott signalled to Andrea to rustle up tea for them, which she rushed off to do.

"It wasn't enough, Inspector. She was gone for a whole day. How could no one have seen her? We're not in the middle of nowhere. Kitty needed to travel along *one* road. How the fuck did no one see her? And now I've lost my little baby..." Hot, salty tears snaked down her face, collecting around her nose and dripping off her lips. "You don't know how it feels. It's like a part of me is gone."

Scott made no reaction, giving Ellen the space to vent her emotions, but he also needed Kitty's mum onside.

"Mrs Morris, I do know how you're feeling. I lost my only

daughter several years ago. She would have been nine. I do understand."

Ellen looked up, pain etched in her features, as her puffy and sore eyes connected with Scott.

Their shared pain seemed to quieten the woman. She turned her head and stared off into the distance, nodding slightly, lost in her thoughts. "How did Kitty die?"

"She fell from a bridge. We are not sure why she was up there." Ellen closed her eyes and pursed her lips.

"Did Kitty have any problems? Perhaps troubles at school or problems at home?"

"Not that I'm aware of, Inspector. She didn't enjoy school; studying wasn't one of her strengths. I occasionally got a call from the school to say Kitty hadn't done her homework or that she had given the teachers a bit of backchat. But having watched documentaries about schools in Yorkshire and Manchester, it looked like that was normal."

"Anything else?"

"She got into trouble a few times. A bit of name-calling, girls slagging off each other. Kitty got a couple of detentions for that, and for not turning in her homework. But nothing more serious."

It was a difficult subject but Scott needed to ask. He shot a glance at Helen, raising his brow as if to suggest: *here I go... light the touchpaper and stand back.*

"How was her relationship with you and her dad? Were there any problems there?"

Scott's question resulted in Ellen firing back a piercing, cold glare. "What are you suggesting, Inspector? That my husband and I were partially responsible for this? That we weren't good parents?"

Scott raised a hand to pacify the woman. "Not at all, Mrs

Morris. I'm trying to build a better picture of family life. I understand you're both working parents, so I'm curious to know how you made that work with being there for Kitty."

"We managed. And we loved Kitty. Please don't think we had anything to do with our daughter's death." Her words were clipped and direct.

Scott moved on, clearly having touched a nerve. He asked Ellen about Kitty's friends, and what mood she was in when she left for school yesterday morning. The picture he was building of Kitty's home life was good. She didn't enjoy school much and kept her friendship circle small, primarily hanging out with two girls, Claudia White and Mia Boswell. Nothing suggested she'd had problems.

"Did she ever talk to you about being bullied?" Scott asked, watching for the woman's reactions and where her eyes travelled.

Ellen furrowed her brow. "Bullying? My God, do you think that led to her death? No... No... That can't be true."

"Mrs Morris, I'm not suggesting that for a minute. I'm trying to cover all angles, and I don't know whether she had mentioned anything in the past to you?"

Her eyes travelled to the ceiling, as she searched her visual memories for anything she may have overlooked in conversations with Kitty in the past. Then, she shook her head and grief consumed her again.

Scott added, "If it's okay with you, I'd like to look around her bedroom?"

Ellen said she was happy for him to do so, and Scott left Helen with her, just as Andrea came back with a tray of teas.

Scott made his way up the stairs and soon located Kitty's room. He snapped on a pair of latex gloves before entering. It was a typical teenager's room with piles of clothes – clean or dirty – strewn across the floor. A big TV sat on a chest of drawers. A makeup box lay open on the floor, filled with an assortment of naked colour palettes, brushes, and false lashes. A string of fairy lights had been sellotaped around the headboard of her bed, and a large mirror hung from the wall, its frame encrusted with brightly coloured jewels. He peered into her wardrobes and noticed various hoodies, long-sleeve tops, and drainpipe jeans hanging up.

It was easy to build a picture of Kitty. She liked the urban look with Nike hoodies, an assortment of baseball caps, misguided jeans, and several pairs of Nike trainers, sitting as prized possessions in their boxes at the bottom of the wardrobe. Scott peered under her mattress and then under the bed to see if anything had been hidden. He found nothing but empty sweet wrappers and scrunched up bits of paper which, when examined, turned out to be failed attempts at homework Kitty had drawn lines through.

Next step would be to instruct uniformed officers to conduct a thorough search of her bedroom first thing in the morning.

Scott was about to leave the room when he decided to open the first drawer on a bedside cabinet. It was stuffed with socks, but something at the back of the drawer piqued his interest. A silver necklace with a heart-shaped pendant, along with eighty pounds in cash. He placed both in separate, clear evidence bags before heading downstairs.

When he returned, Helen was crouching next to Ellen, gently stroking her hand.

"Mrs Morris, do you recognise either of these?" Scott asked, holding up the bags.

Ellen studied both and shook her head. "The necklace

isn't something we bought her. Perhaps one of her friends did?"

"Is there any reason why she would hide this and the cash at the back of her sock drawer?" Scott asked. "Kitty had a jewellery box by her television containing other jewellery. I wonder why it wasn't in there?"

Ellen didn't have an answer.

"Did she get pocket money?"

"A fiver a week. So, I'm not sure where she got four twenty-pound notes from. If her dad had given her money, I would have known about it. We always agree on things like pocket money," Ellen replied, looking puzzled.

"Did she have a boyfriend?" Helen asked, as she continued to rub Ellen's hand.

"She did, once. A boy called Adam from her school. They hung around together for about a year. The usual thing... young love. They were inseparable, did everything together. I lost count of the number of times he was here. They would crash on the sofa with a big bag of Doritos and a bottle of Coke and watch something on Netflix after school. I didn't mind that. If she was indoors, then I knew she was safe."

"And what happened?" Helen prompted.

"The usual thing. It fizzled out. It's never really serious at that age, is it? But I think Kitty was more hurt than Adam. I remember her coming home in tears, throwing her bags on the floor and stomping up to her bedroom. When I followed her up there, she was fuming. Apparently, Adam was already knocking around with another girl within weeks of them splitting up. That made Kitty feel even worse. But I guess it's part of the journey they go through, as kids I mean?" Ellen suggested, as she looked between Scott and Helen.

Scott finished his questioning not long after, giving Ellen the space to come to terms with her loss.

As he drove off with Helen, he eyed the two evidence bags he had placed on the dashboard. Why had Kitty buried these things at the back of her drawer?

7

The rear parking sensors bleeped furiously as Scott reversed into his allocated parking space; the tone grew louder and faster as his rear bumper inched closer to the car behind him.

Scott let out a sigh of exasperation. Parking in Hove was getting more limited with residents gobbling up any available spaces. Despite that frustration, it was a great place to live, close to the buzz and vibrancy of town, but in a calmer and more relaxed area.

Scott switched off the ignition and stared out at the darkness. Residents on his street were safely tucked up inside their houses; families were camped around the TV enjoying normal family life. If they only knew what he saw on a day-to-day basis, they'd realise that life wasn't so rosy. The horrors he'd witnessed today would be branded into his mind, never to be erased. No wonder so many officers ended up on long-term sick leave or quit the force with PTSD. They constantly witnessed the worst of society, the worst of human behaviour, and the pain of grief and tragedy.

His windscreen began to steam up from his anger, and he knew it was his cue to leave.

He stepped out of the car and looked up and down the length of the road, still lost in his thoughts. There was nothing but peace and tranquillity – if only that was the case within his own mind. Sometimes his world felt too surreal and he hated the job. Death was always a hard thing to cope with, and it was challenging at the best of times when dealing with an adult death in suspicious circumstances. He would never get used to dealing with juvenile deaths, let alone those involving infants. Thankfully, he hadn't experienced many of those, but he'd known colleagues who had needed professional counselling after dealing with infant homicides.

Scott tried so hard to wash away the dreadful images of Kitty from his mind, but no matter which direction he looked in – at the surrounding houses, the beautiful architecture and colourful gardens and hedges – the pretty images were torn from his view, replaced by the mangled and twisted remains of Kitty Morris. He would never forget her vacant, staring eyes. He wondered what she'd felt as the road had hurtled towards her.

Why was he doing this to himself? *Fuck. Stop.*

What was he going to gain from replaying that scene on an endless loop?

Scott dragged his weary body up his garden path and put the key in the lock. Warmth hit him when he stepped into the hallway. He dropped his case at the bottom of the stairs and hung his coat up before following the sounds of the TV through to the lounge.

Cara was curled up on the sofa in her pyjamas, with a

thick, fluffy, blue dressing gown that made her look all warm and snuggly. She looked over her shoulder as Scott entered the room.

"Oh babes, you look shattered."

Scott flopped down beside her. He dropped his head back and let it sink into the soft, inviting cushions. There was an empty wine glass and a bottle of wine on the table in front of him, but he didn't have the energy to pour himself a glass. From the looks of it, Cara had worked her way through one glass already.

"I am. It's days like this that leave you feeling like an empty shell."

Cara pressed a gentle kiss to his cheek before pouring Scott a glass and handing it to him.

The first few sips hit the spot and loosened his muscles. "What a day."

"How did things go?" Cara asked, genuinely concerned. She had seen Scott like this on many occasions and had come to expect that his mind would, on occasion, be clouded in confusion and emotional turmoil.

"We didn't make a lot of progress today but that's to be expected. I can't shake the images of Kitty from my mind. I know everyone has their own way of dealing with it, but these kinds of incidents always get to me. I know I need to stay objective, and I know her parents have had their world turned upside down and God I know how that feels, but..." Scott stared up at the ceiling, lost for words.

Cara pulled Scott into her and held him tight. She kissed the side of his head and stroked his face. He breathed in her scent, familiar and comforting. He could stay locked in her embrace forever and nothing else would matter.

"I saw the dad earlier," Cara said. "I wasn't really comfortable with him turning up so soon, as we hadn't prepared her. But we shrouded her body, and covered most of her head, leaving only her face exposed. Neil had done a fantastic job with little notice. But I guess it was the least we could do." She whispered, "I'll never forget his piercing cry."

Scott nodded. "The mum is in bits, understandably. I didn't really get much from my visit other than build a better picture of Kitty. But I did discover a necklace and eighty pounds in cash hidden at the back of her sock drawer. So that's worth me following up." Scott offered the salient points, not wishing to give her chapter and verse of his visit. He knew Cara could fill in the blanks.

"I made dinner for you, but it's probably gone cold now. Sorry, I wasn't too sure what time you'd be home. I can heat it up for you now whilst you grab a shower? It will be ready when you come down."

Scott turned to Cara and studied her features. There was warmth and understanding in her dark eyes. She was compassionate and giving, always putting others first. As she traced her finger along the edge of his face from his jaw line to his chin, his body released to an even deeper level of relaxation. He felt safe, wanted, and loved.

"What have I done to deserve you, Cara?"

She offered a soft smile. "I think I should be asking you that, really. For once, I'm with a man I love, a man who trusts and respects me. And above all else, a man who lets me into his heart."

Scott's eyes began to moisten. He couldn't have put it better himself, because that's how he felt for her too.

The journey they were on was both exciting and fulfilling. He was grateful for her understanding, consideration, and support. Scott had learnt a valuable lesson being with Cara. He didn't need to be rich, or have a big friendship circle, or have the most expensive car or house, or even compete for her attention or affection. It was about sharing life and laughter. And today of all days, he wouldn't have wanted to come home to an empty house.

8

The aroma of warm coffee wafted up and stirred Scott's senses. It kept him grounded in the moment, even though the events of yesterday still played heavily on his mind.

He watched TV downstairs, a random breakfast show where presenters were sharing an amusing story. Though his eyes were fixed on the screen, his mind wandered. The caffeine was doing its job but taking bloody ages.

"Penny for your thoughts?" Cara's voice broke his trance.

"Shit, sorry. I didn't know you'd woken. Are you okay?"

Cara stood behind the sofa and leant over the back, wrapping her arms around his chest. She nuzzled his neck. "I'm fine. More to the point how are you?"

"Firing on all cylinders," he replied, hoisting his mug of coffee in the air.

"You're a crap liar, Scottie."

She could read him so well. Scott's mind had drifted back to Helen's comments after they'd left Ellen Morris. Helen had admitted how she'd wanted to reach out and hug

Kitty's mum. She'd wanted to promise her they'd find out what had happened.

Scott and Cara had breakfast together before leaving for work. He agreed to see her later for the post-mortem.

THE OFFICE WAS quiet by the time Scott arrived. It gave him time alone with his thoughts. Not that he needed it. A restless night had given him too much of that.

After going through his emails and checking the case file online, Scott dropped off the evidence bags from yesterday for Matt's team to analyse, with instructions to check for prints, fibres, and DNA trace evidence. Abby wasn't due in for another hour. Her starting times had been pushed back to give her the opportunity to get the kids ready for school.

By now, Raj and Mike were in but doing little work. Mike had a fixed stare on his face as he leant back in his chair and looked up at the strip light above his head. Raj on the other hand was more animated, scoffing the biggest Danish pastry Scott had seen.

"Raj, I think you're eating breakfast, lunch, and dinner all in one go. There's enough for the whole team in that portion."

"It's just a bit of breakfast, guv," Raj offered in defence, wiping flakes of pastry from the corner of his mouth.

Scott shook his head in disbelief. "Little doesn't even come into the equation. If you carry on eating that much, you'll end up like Mike."

"I think that's a bit unfair, guv. This, I'll have you know," Mike protested, scowling and rubbing his swollen belly, "is what is classed as a dad bod. Believe it or not, women love it."

Raj choked on his pastry as he laughed. Bits of Danish flew across the table before he could place a hand over his mouth.

"Seriously, it's like feeding time at the zoo when I look at either of you," Scott said in mock disgust, glancing at Raj's desk. "Clean yourself up, Raj, or I'll be putting you on a diet of carrot sticks and celery."

"Oh my God," Mike shouted. "Helen the hippie has got to you, guv. She's converted you to the dark side. Next, you'll be having herbal teas and couscous flapjacks, or some shit like that."

"I feel my ears burning," Helen shouted across the floor, as she breezed in through the door.

"Talking of Satan..." Mike snorted.

Scott laughed as Helen joined them, slipping a bag off her shoulder, and placing her breakfast on the desk. "Mike was being very complimentary about you."

Helen narrowed her eyes and viewed Mike with suspicion.

"What's for breakfast?" Mike enquired.

Helen dropped into her chair and whipped the lid off her takeaway cup. "An infused green tea, and a yoghurt granola," she said proudly with a smile.

Mike threw his arms up in the air. "I rest my case."

"I give up with you lot. It's like being back in primary school," Scott remarked. "Let's get back to business. What have we done so far?"

Helen was the first to respond, keen to get in before Mike – much to his disdain. "I've been checking Kitty's social media profiles. As the skip thought, she had an Instagram and TikTok account. She hadn't posted anything on TikTok but was following quite a few people. She was more active on Instagram. There were ninety-seven posts, mainly of her and her friends pulling faces. Random dance shuffle challenges and stuff like that, but I couldn't see anything of concern."

"What about followers?" Scott asked.

"She had four hundred and seventy-seven, and she was following one thousand, five hundred and seventy-four people."

Scott whistled before asking Helen to check each of those profiles. He appreciated it was going to be a laborious task, so he instructed her to rope in a couple of other bodies to check them, to speed things up.

"What about phone records and GPS tracking?" he asked next.

Mike and Raj were sharing that responsibility, but Mike confirmed they were still in the process of downloading the phone logs and would have the data later that morning. The phone triangulation work was still ongoing.

Scott updated the whiteboard. "Helen, can you do me a favour, go back and check on Kitty's mum? I spoke to Andrea this morning, and she said Ellen's behaviour became more erratic and desperate as the evening wore on. Andrea wasn't comfortable leaving her on her own, so she slept on the sofa. Unfortunately, Andrea had to call out a doctor during the night."

Helen nodded in between mouthfuls of her breakfast.

"Oh, and whilst you're there, officers should be arriving to do a detailed sweep of Kitty's bedroom. Before they get there, can you give it the once-over, in case I missed anything?"

"Will do, guv."

"Raj, can you visit Kitty's headmistress? Find out as much as you can about Kitty. How she was getting on at school? Whether she had any problems? When I spoke with her mum last night, she said Kitty didn't enjoy school. She'd had a few detentions over not returning her homework in time, as well as a few run-ins with other girls."

Raj nodded as he jotted down a few points before picking up the phone and calling the school to make an appointment.

Scott thanked them for the update and headed off to update Meadows, who was at his desk and finishing a phone call when Scott appeared in the doorway. Meadows waved him in and gestured for him to take a seat as he wrapped up the conversation.

"Morning, Scott. Busy day yesterday, I gather?"

Meadows was his usual direct self.

"Morning, sir. Yes, you could say that. Busy and challenging. How was the conference?"

"Interesting. It was about modernising the criminal justice system, but it's been a topic of discussion for years, and the cogs of change are slow, so I doubt we'll get anything good from it." His tone was dismissive.

"Still, at least it's being discussed and on the agenda. That's a good thing, right?"

"Possibly, Scott. There were breakout groups to discuss individual aspects of the change process. And each little group was being chaired by a super from a different region. I have to admit, I could have done a better job than many of them. The discussion I was involved in descended into shambles."

Scott tried his hardest to hide a smirk. *That's the reason Meadows isn't rating the conference.*

His ego had taken a bashing because he hadn't been asked to chair one of the breakout groups. With an opportunity to be centre of attention, and have everyone hanging on his every word, he would have relished the attention.

"Never mind, their loss. Where are we with this case?" Meadows asked, bringing his focus back to business.

Scott updated him on the scene they had witnessed and his visit to the parents last night. "I've got the post-mortem later on today. I'm not sure what we'll be able to take from it, but at the moment we are discussing two theories, whether it was suicide or a prank that went wrong."

"What's your first instinct telling you?"

Scott blew out his cheeks. "If I'm honest, I'm not entirely sure. If it was a prank, then the chances are there would have been other people up there with her, but eyewitness reports don't corroborate that theory."

Meadows nodded as he strummed his fingers on the desk. "You're going with the suicide angle?"

"I'm kind of swinging in that direction at the moment."

"Well, we need to concentrate on her home and school life to begin with. That's where I'd start if I was you, Scott."

Scott wanted to shout at Meadows for stating the obvious. Instead, he politely smiled and nodded in agreement, raising a brow.

Meadows continued. "In my experience and when I was a DI like you, I noticed suicides were often linked to relationship problems, either an unhappy home life, problems with their peers, or even bullying. Start there and see how you get on."

Scott couldn't bear this condescending drivel any longer.

He promised to update Meadows shortly as he made his escape.

As Scott walked along the corridor and back downstairs to CID, he shook his head in disbelief. Meadows always got to him. The phrase "don't try to teach your grandmother to suck eggs" sprung to mind.

Abby was in the office by the time Scott returned. She was busy checking for any updates on her computer. A sense of calmness was restored when she smiled up at him as he perched on her desk.

"Morning, Abby. How are you today? Everything good at home?"

"Yes, guv." She laughed. "Apart from two teenage brats arguing over who could have the last Rice Krispies and who had first dibs on the bathroom, everything is fantastic."

Scott smiled. Even though Abby moaned about her kids, like she moaned about everything, he knew she relished every moment with them. This whole, work-life balance scenario they were working through was proving to be a good thing. Abby didn't look as weary or gaunt as she used to. She had a bit more spring in her step, and above all else, she laughed a bit more.

"Right, Abby. I'm off to meet Matt back at the scene. I want to go through a few things with him. You're more than welcome to come along for the ride, as the rest of the team seem to have everything under control. It's up to you?"

Abby hastily pushed her chair back and bent forward to lock her PC screen. "You don't have to ask twice. I'm there."

9

"This skinny latte is a bit cold," Abby muttered, as she took a sip.

Scott rolled his eyes and clipped in his seat belt. He had pulled over on their way to the viaduct to grab two hot drinks, since they would be standing around in the cold. "Do you want me to go back in and ask them to reheat it for you?"

Abby shook her head and tutted. "Nah, it's fine. I've come to the decision most cafés can't make a decent latte, let alone a hot one."

Scott knew better than to argue with Abby. It was one of her pet peeves along with the cold weather, soggy sandwiches, dirty cutlery in restaurants, touching door handles and stair rails, not getting to the gym often enough – and well, most things in life. Moving to safer ground, he updated Abby on feedback from the team, shared in her absence.

"News spread around the school quickly when the headmistress made the announcement about Kitty. Naturally, there was a degree of panic and upset amongst the pupils.

We've assigned PCSOs outside the gates to reassure parents, and deal with any questions they have."

"I don't envy their task. They'll be bombarded," Abby remarked.

Scott agreed. News of the death of a child was always reacted to badly by pupils and their families, but a death in suspicious circumstances only intensified such concerns. That was part of the reason he had sent Raj up to the school. Scott wanted to not only find out more about Kitty but also to give the headmistress reassurances. Having a member from the investigation team would go some way towards providing that comfort.

"I'll tell you what bothers me, Abby. The school confirmed all pupils had left the site by three fifty-five p.m. and there were no after-school events and yet, no one saw Kitty leave. Her friends and history teacher confirmed she was in the last class of the day which ended at three twenty p.m., so where did she go?"

"No sightings of her at the gate?"

"Nope."

"Have we been able to confirm whether she left through the front gates at all?" Abby questioned.

"Unfortunately not. We can't even confirm if she left the school grounds. The school doesn't have cameras positioned at the gates. For some daft reason, they have cameras over-looking the staff car park."

Abby laughed. "That's plain ridiculous. Anyone would think they were more worried about having their cars nicked than the safety of their pupils."

"Exactly," Scott agreed. "We've still got a lot more to do. I've requested a search team do a more extensive sweep of the school grounds, both inside and out."

"Well, hopefully the door-to-door enquiries with shops and residents along her route might throw up something," Abby said, sighing.

Scott caught the abruptness in Abby's tone. He watched her for a few moments as she stared out of her window. "What's up with you today, grumpy drawers?"

"Nothing," she replied flatly.

"Come on. I can tell when something is bothering you. Spit it out."

Abby blew out her cheeks. "I'm just a bit pissed off. I feel like I'm missing out. The whole team were in this morning and you had a team update without me."

Scott smiled. Abby loved being in the thick of everything. She was meticulous in her job, and her OCD tendencies meant she wanted to be in control of everything.

"Abby, you didn't miss anything. I've updated you now on everything we spoke about. Or at least, the important bits."

"Yes, I know," she snapped.

He ignored her harshness and carried on. "Look at how things are for you at the moment. Your morning routines are better, the kids are happier, and you have something resembling normal family life in the mornings and evenings. The balance is much better. And that's what you wanted. If I'm honest, that's what I wanted for you, too."

Abby huffed and grumbled under her breath. It wasn't the briefings or updates which Abby missed but the chit-chat that went along with them.

As the magnificent arches of the Victorian viaduct loomed into view, the brick monolith reaching into the sky almost split the road in two. Scott found a convenient place to park up. Exiting his car, he noticed a small police presence, as inquiries continued. The traffic ran as normal; the remains of the tragic incident had been washed away by council staff, with residents and shopkeepers going about their usual business. Several blue police signs were positioned along the pavement on both sides, alerting the locals to an incident that had taken place here, with the date and time, and a request for anyone with information to come forward.

Scott stood for a moment, taking in the view of the viaduct. Abby stood alongside him. His eyes travelled to the top as he pictured Kitty standing on the edge.

Sensing what Scott must have been thinking, Abby took in the height of the drop. "There was no chance of survival – not for anyone."

They were shaken from their own thoughts and reflections when Matt joined them. "Ah, there you are, Scott, Abby. I've had a team on site here for most of yesterday. We faced particular problems in gaining access to the top of the viaduct. The BTP boys finally gained clearance, once Southern Rail agreed to close the line. The railway bosses were a bit pissed off about the two-hour closure, because it caused delays."

"That's their problem, not ours," Scott said.

Matt nodded in agreement. "It was a decent enough window for us to do a forensic search across the whole span of the viaduct. BTP officers accompanied us. They are a funny old lot. They insisted on going everywhere with us, so we put them to good use and had the uniformed officers conduct a fingertip search as well, whilst their detectives stood in serious huddles, scratching their chins and looking important."

The vision brought a smile to Scott's face.

Matt continued. "Their officers believe she gained access

to the top of the viaduct through an empty building over there." He pointed to a boarded-up shop ringed by a wire fence, next to one of the pillars. "It has a two-storey extension at the back, with a flat roof. They discovered two scaffold boards positioned from the roof to an adjoining metal stairwell that engineers use to access the top of the viaduct."

Scott wondered how long the boards had been there. It wasn't uncommon for kids to find different ways to access private property like bridges and railway lines, either to sabotage train services or to sprawl their graffiti across the brick canvases.

Having agreed to catch up with Matt later, Scott and Abby spent a few moments walking up and down the street, milling amongst the crowds, and building a clearer picture of their environment.

Mothers wheeled buggies, keen to get their young ones to nursery. Students ambled along the pavements on their way to lectures, sipping on Red Bull to either fire them up for the day or shake off a hangover from the night before. Scott watched a grocery store owner laying out bowls of fruit and vegetables on trestle tables outside the shop. He created a splash of bright colour with bananas, yellow and red peppers, oranges, and pre-cut slices of watermelon. It was sad at how quickly life returned to normal for most people after a tragedy.

In and amongst normal life, officers from the extended search team darted in and out of stores, continuing to ask questions.

"I'm still unsure of the motive," Abby remarked, as she folded her arms across her chest and scanned the crowd, hoping the little pieces of uncertainty in her mind would come together to form a cohesive insight.

"I know what you mean. I was initially thinking it might have been suicide. But what happened if it was a prank that went wrong?"

Abby turned to Scott and shot him a questioning glance, silently pushing him to elaborate.

"Look at how busy the street is, Abby. Imagine if it was a prank that went wrong? I know eyewitnesses didn't see anyone else up there with Kitty, but others who were in the prank might have been down here watching. They could have scarpered the minute it went wrong. And if that's the case, why didn't anyone see a few kids running away?"

Scott and Abby returned their gazes to the top of the viaduct, more confused than ever.

NEITHER OF THEM was looking forward to their visit to the mortuary. Cara had completed her preliminary and detailed investigations and was finishing recording the last of her dictated notes when Scott and Abby arrived. They gowned up and joined Cara in the examination room.

Kitty's body looked even younger and smaller lying on the examination table. Both officers found it hard to look at her. Abby covered her mouth with her hand, whilst Scott ground his teeth. There wasn't much left of the back of Kitty's head. The impact had been so severe it had shattered her skull, destroyed her brain, and pushed her facial features so far forward, her eyes bulged.

Sensing the emotions both officers felt, Cara stepped back from the table and rested her hands on her hips. "This was a tough one for me, too. Kitty was of average height and weight. There were no marks on her body, and no signs of sexual interference."

"Well, that's good news, and I guess reassuring for the parents," Scott remarked, unable to steal his gaze away from the table.

Cara agreed, nodding in sympathy. "Cause of death was severe trauma to the head. If there's one consolation, she didn't feel any pain."

"Have you done the usual?" Abby whispered, feeling her chest heave. She wasn't sure if she was about to throw up, or whether it was waves of anxiety crashing through her.

"Yep. We've taken tox samples, and scrapings from her mouth, and from under her nails. I've examined her hands and her clothes and there are no grass or mud stains, so she may not have been roughing it in the last twenty-four hours. Her last meal was chips and pizza."

Scott raised a brow. "Timeframe?"

"I'd say around two to four hours before death."

Scott's eyes widened.

Where did Kitty eat the day she died?

It would be an impossible task to check every place that sold pizza and chips, in the hope one of them might have served her and so seen her.

Unless she didn't buy it?

Another thought popped into his mind. *Maybe she ate wherever she'd stayed overnight?*

10

With time working against them, Scott grabbed lunch on the way back to the office before spending the next few hours reviewing the witness statements gathered so far. Of those he read, no one had seen anyone else up on the viaduct apart from Kitty, just before she stepped off the ledge.

Standing by the window in the briefing room now, he looked out into the darkness and the city beyond. His thoughts travelled to Kitty's parents. Andrea, the FLO, had reported both parents were struggling to cope, and that another family had arrived to help out and support them.

He checked his watch and grabbed his phone from the ledge before dialling Cara's number. She picked up.

"Hi, babes, how are you? I thought I'd give you a quick buzz before the evening briefing. The others will be here in a few minutes after Mike wheels in the TV monitor."

"I'm okay, Scottie. I've only been back home an hour or so, so I thought I'd tidy up, as my boyfriend is a real, messy pup."

Scott smiled. She'd done it again, cheered him up effortlessly. It was the lift he needed. "You need to sack him, or at least swap him for a better model."

"Believe me I've tried, but I've scraped the bottom of the barrel with this one, and I doubt there's much better out there."

"You cheeky cow," Scott roared, as Cara cracked up at the other end.

"Will you be long?" she asked.

"Hopefully not. An hour tops. We've got a few things to review, including footage from the buses. Shall I call you when I leave?"

"Sounds good. Please don't work too late. I'm worried you're overdoing it. Shall I make you dinner?"

"I promise I'm fine. And don't worry about food, I'll fix up a sandwich when I get in," Scott reassured her.

Cara sighed and fell silent for a few seconds. "Babes, I'm not happy about that. You need to keep your strength up and living off sandwiches is something you do during the day. You should at least have a proper meal when you come home in the evenings. I'm popping out to the shops in a minute anyway, so I'll pick up a few bits. Any requests?"

"God, you're sounding like my mother," Scott teased.

"Scottie... I'm warning you. What do you want?"

"Okay. Okay. Let me think. I know. I want you. I want you wrapped in a dairy milk wrapper," Scott whispered softly.

"Scottie, don't get me started. You know what I'm like when I get an idea into my head. If I sit here for the next hour thinking about you undressing me, I'll be in bits by the time you arrive. I'll have to distract myself by walking up and down the freezer aisles of Tesco's a dozen times until I've cooled down."

They both laughed. Scott loved their sexy conversations. Just before he hung up, he agreed to text as he was leaving.

As the team filed in, Scott looked out of the window once more. Brighton was in the full throes of winter. Dark mornings and even darker nights heralded the time of year when Brighton was at its coldest.

As they all settled around the table, Raj lightened the mood by opening up a box of French fancies, and a packet of chocolate Bourbons before sliding them into the middle of the table for everyone to tuck into with their cuppas. The sentiment was warmly appreciated as a sea of hands reached into the middle and grabbed at the goodies, their arms flailing like an octopus out of water.

Scott took a few moments to check everyone's mental state. He knew they were finding this case tough, but he repeated the need for them to stay objective. He began by giving the team a quick update on the post-mortem, and the blood and tissue samples sent away for analysis, before turning to Raj for an update on his visit to the headmistress.

Raj put down his half-eaten biscuit before opening his notepad and relaying the salient points. "I had an interesting conversation with the headmistress, Mrs Isabella Glanville. She's fit."

The team laughed.

"And you're saying that because it has a relevance to our case how?" Helen interrupted.

Raj shrugged and moved on sheepishly, avoiding Helen's glare. "As I was saying, it was an interesting conversation. The head painted a colourful picture of Kitty. Lots of potential but easily distracted. She missed homework deadlines – as we know – and had a few detentions – which we know too

– but she was well known for answering back, and giving her teachers hell."

"I feel sorry for teachers. They do get a rough ride," Helen remarked.

"Any issues with attendance?" Abby asked.

Raj grimaced. "On the whole, attendance was good. Isabella checked the records, and Kitty had one long absence for eight days about two months ago. Food poisoning, according to her mum."

"Did you gather much about her friends?" Scott asked.

"Claudia White and Mia Boswell," Raj confirmed, checking his notes.

Though the visit was helpful, it didn't progress the case and that concerned Scott.

Abby put her elbows on the table and rested her chin on both hands. "We're still struggling to map out her movements during the last twenty-four hours. It's not uncommon for kids to go missing. Especially when they've had a barney at home, or when they're feeling a bit low. But most of them come back within a few hours. This doesn't make sense to me. The post-mortem didn't indicate she had been living rough for the last twenty-four hours, or hiding in a derelict building, or in the park, or anything like that. She must have been indoors with someone?"

The thought hung in the air and was met with a few nods. The question on everyone's lips was "where?"

Scott jotted down a few points in his notebook. "Raj, as you've already made contact with the head, I want you to lead on having a chat with both of Kitty's friends first thing tomorrow. Take Helen with you." Scott turned to Helen. "Is that okay with you?"

"Fine with me. It will probably stop him flirting with the

head," Helen said, shooting a glare at Raj that suggested *I'm watching you.* "Whilst we're all here, I might as well give you an update on my visit to see Kitty's mum. She's definitely losing it, and understandably. Her doctor is thinking of giving her a sedative, but Ellen is refusing. I took the opportunity to ask Ellen about her daughter's behaviour, and whether she had noticed any change in it recently."

"And did she?" Scott asked.

"Well, to be honest, her answer was less than helpful. I don't think she's thinking straight. She said Kitty was always in her bedroom and had taken to shouting at her more recently every time she poked her head around the door to check on her. But it's hard to say whether that's a teenage thing or not."

Scott folded his arms and considered the next steps. Mike had already spoken about Kitty's phone logs and GPS location, which indicated that her phone had been switched off at three twenty p.m. on the day of her disappearance. Nothing in her call log warranted concern other than a few calls from an unregistered number, which Mike was looking into.

All other lines of enquiry revealed little of interest. Officers were continuing to trawl through CCTV footage closer to the viaduct. Door-to-door enquiries near the school and on Kitty's route to the park offered nothing new but were ongoing. Many residents had commented that with so many pupils spilling out onto the street, it would be hard to pick out one individual person, and they often saw the pupils moving in large, noisy groups before splitting off in different directions.

There was one final piece of evidence they needed to review, and for this reason Scott had left it until the end of their briefing. It was camera footage taken from a bus approaching the viaduct.

Mike pressed the play button on the remote control. Footage appeared on screen of the street view from the driver's cab, as the bus made its way along the road. In the distance and about one hundred yards ahead, the viaduct came into view. The room fell silent as everyone watched the brutal, final seconds of Kitty's life play out. It felt like they were watching a horror movie. Abby wanted to turn away but forced herself to look, with a hand over her mouth. A small figure could be seen near the top of the screen.

Kitty stood on the ledge, her arms spread out by her sides, and as the bus narrowed the gap to the viaduct, she stared at the sky. There appeared to be no one else with her. As they continued to watch in silence, Kitty leant forward and fell. There was no evidence of her arms and legs flailing out of fear or panic. When she hit the ground, she was parallel to it, with her arms and legs outstretched like a starfish.

Helen sniffed as she wiped away a tear with the back of her hand. Raj hung his head in despair, and Mike shook his head in disbelief.

The impact was catastrophic. From the footage, bystanders and pedestrians stopped in their tracks, unable to comprehend what they had witnessed. Women threw their hands to their faces, others screamed. Several rushed to Kitty's aid, but backed off when they realised there was nothing they could do.

Scott closed his eyes for a second, desperate to hold back the tears that threatened to engulf him.

"Shit," he whispered.

They reviewed a second piece of footage from a car dash

cam. The car was approaching the viaduct from the opposite direction. Viewing it from a different angle only confirmed their thoughts. They sat in silence for a few minutes, alone with their own emotions, respectful and saddened.

Abby pulled a tissue from her pocket and blew her nose. "That looked like suicide to me. The evidence suggests as much. What was affecting her life so much that she needed to end it?" She muttered, blowing her nose again.

"That's what we need to find out, Abby," Scott replied. "I want you all to go home. It's been a tough day. We need an early night. First thing tomorrow, I want you to double your efforts to look into Kitty's life in greater detail. A child doesn't just happen to scale a seventy-foot viaduct and then leap off it. Witnesses didn't hear a scream, nor did anyone spot her loitering up there for any length of time. This doesn't add up. We could be looking at suicide, or something more suspicious. Check her parents and the relationship she had with them. Then find out if she had any problems at school. Was she being bullied? Was she struggling to make friends? Was she under any kind of peer pressure? Find the answers."

11

Scott watched Cara, still fast asleep, as he buttoned up his shirt. He felt a warm glow inside which left him with a contented smile. Despite his insistence on making a sandwich when he'd got in last night, Cara had gone to the trouble of picking up lasagne for them, and adding baby new potatoes, honey roasted carrots, and peas. They had finished their meal together with a slice of cheesecake and filter coffee. There were no limits to what Cara would do for him, and he felt thoroughly spoilt.

She had been so insistent about him eating a proper meal that the minute he'd walked through the front door, she had ordered him to take off his jacket and set the dining table. Cara had refused to entertain any of his ifs and buts.

He'd loved everything about last night, including the lovemaking afterwards. As he looked at her now, she looked so peaceful and sweet, with the duvet wrapped up under her chin. Even asleep, she looked stunning. He leant across the bed and kissed her on the forehead, breathing in her scent as he buried his nose in her hair.

Christmas had only been a few weeks ago, and memories of their time together flooded into his thoughts. They'd decided it would be the two of them for their first Christmas. Cara had been so considerate and thoughtful. She knew how hard this time of year was for him and had made a real fuss of him. Whilst cooking Christmas lunch, she had told him to go to the cemetery to lay flowers for Tina and Becky and have a quiet moment with the family he still loved so much. As he'd hugged Cara, he'd fought hard to hold back the tears.

Just recalling the time moistened his eyes. It had been a selfless act of love he'd never forget. She had been so understanding, especially when he'd returned from the cemetery to find her waiting in the hallway. Warmth and understanding had flowed through every pore of her being while she'd held him for ages, not moving, and not saying anything. Just being there for him.

Having not yet even been together for a year, Cara's impact on his life was profound. They worked well together, personally and professionally. Emotionally, she was tuned in to his thoughts, his feelings and moods without him having to utter a word. Being with her was the happiest he had felt in many years. He kissed her again and headed downstairs.

Scott had just put away his papers in his case and polished off his last piece of toast, slathered in butter, when Cara came down in her dressing gown.

"You should have woken me..." she mumbled, her throat croaky and dry.

Scott wrapped his arms around her. "You looked too warm and snuggly. I didn't want to disturb you."

"You're kidding me, right? I'm not going to miss an opportunity to say goodbye to my man," she replied, planting a soft kiss on his lips. She stared deep into his eyes. "You do know that I love you, Scottie?"

Scott smiled in return. "I'm kind of getting that impression, yeah. And I love you just as much. You're the reason I look forward to coming home in the evenings."

Cara undid the cord on her dressing gown, allowing it to gape and reveal her naked flesh. "I don't suppose you've got time for another breakfast, have you?"

Scott shook his head in consternation. "You're going to get me sacked one day."

"At least when that day comes, you'll have a smile on your face."

CAUSEWAY SECONDARY SCHOOL was tucked away in the northern end of Hove, hidden from the street by a six-foot box hedge that skirted its boundary at the front. The rumble of traffic from the A27 confirmed the rear boundary of the school field was no more than a few hundred metres away from the flow of traffic.

"This takes me back a bit," Raj whispered, as he and Helen were escorted from the front reception towards Mrs Glanville's office.

The corridor walls had exposed, natural brickwork, with noticeboards spaced at random intervals. A familiar smell of ageing wood desks, school canteen smells, and the echo of hundreds of footsteps brought back nostalgic memories, both good and bad. Helen jumped when a buzzer went off, signalling the start of the first lesson. They weaved in and out of kids who scurried like busy ants, heading from their form rooms to classes. The sound of dozens of frenetic conversations soon filled the space.

The head was waiting for them in a doorway as they arrived. Isabella Glanville introduced herself to Helen and showed the officers through to her office. Helen rolled her eyes when she saw Raj grinning at the headmistress, whilst leaning back and trying to look all smooth and confident.

"Thank you for taking the time to organise this for us, Mrs Glanville," Raj began. "We appreciate you're busy, and we don't want to keep Mia and Claudia out of their lessons for too long, so can we crack on?"

Isabella gave them a reassuring smile and nod. "Of course. It's an upsetting time for all of us, so I would appreciate it if you could be discreet and sympathetic with your interviews. I run a tight school here, and I like to believe my teaching staff and I have a good handle on our pupils' welfare." Mrs Glanville adjusted a few papers on her desk as she tidied up. "There's not a lot that gets past us, and we have gained the trust of our student population. I'd like to think that if anything was bothering them, they'd come and see me or one of the teaching staff. My door is always open to them, and I'd like it to still be the case after you leave. After all, they're the next generation and we have a duty to guide and support them for their futures."

"That's good to hear," Raj said. He wondered how many times she'd reeled off that polished pitch at the school open evening.

"Where would you like to conduct them? You're more than welcome to use my office, and I can sit outside, in case you need me."

"Absolutely, Mrs Glanville. We don't want to upset the girls any further. It would be fantastic if we can use this office because it's out of the way, and the girls won't feel so intimidated. And because they are minors, we'd appreciate it if you could stay inside the room as an appropriate adult, and perhaps sit at the back?"

Isabella agreed that it would be a sensible thing to do and left the room to fetch Mia. She returned a few minutes later with Mia in tow and asked the girl to take a seat in front of her desk. She introduced the officers to her before heading to the back of the room and planting herself in a spare seat.

"Hi, Mia. I'm Raj and this is Helen," Raj began, nodding in Helen's direction. "We're looking into the sad accident your friend Kitty was involved in and wanted to ask you a few questions, if that's okay?"

Mia was tight-lipped, her big, round, brown eyes flicking between Raj and Helen. Both officers continued to smile, hoping it would relax her.

The girl nodded, but looked terrified, her hands scrunched in a tight ball and buried deep in her lap. "Like what?"

"We are just trying to build a picture of Kitty's life. What she liked, what she didn't like, even the friends she had," Raj added for reassurance.

Mia shrugged her shoulders in reply.

Raj groaned inwardly, sensing it would be hard pulling any details or facts from the girl. "We understand you were really good friends with Kitty. Can you tell us a little about her?"

Mia cleared her throat, her hands clenching even tighter. "She was a friend. We hung around together, not so much in school, but mainly afterwards because we were in different forms and at different ends of the school."

"Who did she hang around with in school?"

"Claudia."

"Claudia White?" Raj asked for confirmation, to which Mia nodded. "Did you hang out in particular places?"

Mia shrugged, the way most kids of her age did when they had little to say.

"Mia?" Helen chipped in with a soft prompt.

"Mainly outside the chippy and Stop Out. There aren't many other places to hang out around here. It's a dump."

Helen looked at Isabella at the back of the room. She rolled her eyes and shook her head.

"Were there any kids from other schools who met there?" Raj continued.

"A few. We all know each other through Snapchat and Insta."

"Was there any trouble between kids from your school and other schools?"

Mia fell silent and stared at her lap before changing tack to glance around the room. She avoided making eye contact with the officers.

Raj and Helen tried to persuade her to open up, but their efforts appeared to fall on deaf ears when she offered little more than a shrug of her shoulders. Even a prompt from Isabella proved unsuccessful.

"Do you know much about the boyfriend she once had?" Raj checked his notes. "Adam?"

Mia nodded, giving the most basic of details about the boy. The officers gleaned he was Adam Minor, a year-eleven pupil, and someone Kitty had briefly been involved with. Helen asked Isabella to summon Adam for a quick chat, too. She left the room briefly to instruct her secretary before re-joining the interview.

After that brief interruption, Raj pushed on. "Mia, it's really important. Did Kitty ever mention that she was in trouble or upset about anything? Was she meeting someone?"

Mia shook her head violently. Too violently.

Helen leant forward, rested her elbows on her thighs, and placed her hands together. "Mia, this is really important. Kitty's parents are so upset. They really want answers and want to know why their little girl ended up in such a terrible accident. It doesn't matter how small or insignificant you think a detail is, but anything you know could be really valuable to us. I promise you, this conversation is completely confidential, and you're not in trouble."

Mia chewed on her lower lip. "No, she didn't tell me anything."

"She wasn't being bullied?"

Mia shook her head.

"Are you sure?"

Mia nodded.

"When you were with Kitty, did anyone ever try to sell you drugs, or give you money, or anything of that nature?"

When Mia stonewalled them again, the interview didn't continue for much longer. Her reluctance to answer and avoid questions meant neither Raj nor Helen were making much of a headway. Isabella apologised on behalf of Mia, a touch of embarrassment and frustration in her tone.

They didn't fare much better in their interview with Adam Minor. A sixteen-year-old adolescent with an attitude, he presented himself as a tough, confident individual, unnerved by nothing. Sprouting the first signs of extra hair growth on his upper lip, he described his relationship with Kitty as nothing more than a bit of fun – as if he were well versed in relationships – and said that girls came and went.

As previously confirmed by Kitty's mother, Adam commented that Kitty seemed to be more upset with their split than him. She had hounded him for a few weeks with text messages, leaving voicemails of her crying, begging him to meet her to talk. He'd callously ignored all of her messages, which had only upset her further. His recollections brought a smile to his smug face.

Adam's nonchalant attitude towards relationships grated on Helen, and it didn't go unnoticed that his clothes carried a subtle smell of cigarette smoke. Helen concluded the interview early, realising Adam was offering nothing of value. He was an individual who played the field, and as soon as he realised girls wanted him, now enjoyed the buzz and the notoriety of being one of the most popular boys in the year.

Raj and Helen took a five-minute break to stretch their legs and call Abby to update her on the slow progress of the interviews. During the break, Isabella left the room to chase up Claudia White. Through the open door, Raj saw Isabella speaking to her secretary in a hushed whisper, concerned expressions etched in both of their features.

Isabella rushed back into her office to tell the officers that Claudia hadn't turned up for registration that morning. Her secretary had spoken to her form teacher and then to Claudia's mother, who confirmed Claudia left for school this morning at eight fifteen, as normal. Attempts by her mother and the school to contact her by phone had proved unsuccessful so far.

"Could she have bunked off?" Raj suggested.

Isabella rushed out of the room again to check the online

attendance register with her secretary before returning. She confirmed Claudia had never been late for school before.

Raj exchanged an uncomfortable look with Helen as he weighed up the evidence in his own mind.

Does she know something about Kitty's death? Or has something more sinister happened to her?

12

The moment Scott walked in the office he felt the tension. Phones were ringing off the hook, uniformed officers were moving around desks, and Abby was pacing the floor in a heightened state of alertness.

"What's happening, Abby?" Scott frowned, as he looked around CID on the way to his office.

Abby strode after him. "Claudia White didn't show up for school this morning."

"And she's not accounted for?" Scott asked, dropping his case by the side of his desk and taking off his jacket, before hanging it on the back of his chair.

"No. We've got Raj and Helen at the school and I have asked them to stay there for the time being. They were conducting interviews with Kitty's friends, and Claudia was the next on their list, but she didn't turn up for school." Abby continued to fill him in on how the interviews had gone.

"Fuck. This is all we need. What have we done so far?"

"The school has tried Claudia's mobile number a few

times, as has her mum. It's going through to voicemail. We've put in a request for a signal trace. If it's on, we'll have location data for her. We've got uniformed officers in the process of organising a MisPer report. I've tried her number as well, guv, without any joy."

"Any feedback from the mum in terms of Claudia's behaviour this morning?" Scott asked, following Abby out onto the CID floor and heading for the whiteboard.

Abby confirmed Claudia had appeared normal when she'd left for school. Her mum had started to panic, with each message left on Claudia's mobile becoming more desperate.

"Guv, I've drafted in extra officers to trace her route to school because she is a minor."

"This isn't good news. Three friends at school. One is dead, one is missing, and the third is uncooperative." Scott examined the whiteboard with Kitty's picture on it. Pictures of Mia and Claudia had been pinned alongside hers. He turned his focus on pictures of Claudia. "I'd like to say she will probably be picked up within the hour, but my gut instinct is telling me something else. We need to categorise this one as a high-risk priority."

Abby nodded in agreement. "I suggest we send Raj and Helen to speak to Claudia's mum. They are not far away, and it would be good if we moved quickly."

Scott agreed, with the instruction that either Raj or Helen report in as soon as they had concluded their visit.

Mike rose from his chair and moved alongside Scott and Abby.

"We've got more intel from the door-to-door enquiries. Officers have extended their search to cover Hangleton Park and the surrounding area. It is in the opposite direction to where Kitty should have been heading to meet her mum." Mike jabbed his chubby finger on the map pinned to the whiteboard and circled the search area. "There's a parade of shops on Kitty's walk home. Billy Crowther, a shop assistant at Stop Out, recognised Kitty's photograph. There is a chip shop along that parade as well, called Oh My Cod, and the owner, Kristos Barros, recognised Kitty's picture as well."

Scott studied the street map and its proximity to both the school and Kitty's route home. "This area has already come up in earlier conversations. What do we know about it?"

Mike checked his notes before continuing. "It's a regular stop-off for lots of the kids who pick up a portion of chips or a box of fried chicken on their way home from school. It's like the regular hangout place."

"Kitty's last known movements could have been in this area..." Scott speculated.

Mike shrugged a shoulder. "Possibly. Both Billy and Kristos commented they hadn't seen her on the day she disappeared, but she was there often."

"Okay, Mike, good work. Keep digging for me. Abby and I will take a trip there now."

IT WAS an unusual location for a small parade of shops, but its popularity was evident from the discarded sweet wrappers, chip cones, and fried chicken boxes over spilling from two litter bins. Scott had parked up the road and walked the remaining distance, to build up a visual layout of the area. The parade featured an assortment of shops, with a convenience store at one end and an electrical supplies store, chip shop, hairdresser, and a retro arcade outlet at the other.

"I've not seen a shop like this in a long time," Scott remarked to Abby, as they stood outside Stop Out.

It was a retro arcade shop where kids could play old arcade machines like Space Invaders, Street Fighter, and Pacman. Memories flooded back for Scott as he stepped through the doorway and into the darkened space beyond. His feet stuck to the rubber floor. Arcade machines lined both walls, with a counter at the far end. Beside the counter were two chiller cabinets stocked with an assortment of soft drinks. One half of the counter was given over to selling convenience snacks like chocolates, sweets, and crisps. It reminded Scott of a similar place he'd visited during his youth.

The lights had been deliberately dimmed, so the arcade screens showed off their dated graphics.

Scott and Abby made their way towards the back of the shop where they found a young man standing behind the counter. They presented their warrant cards and introduce themselves. "We are looking for Billy Crowther."

"That's me," he said confidently, pulling his shoulders back and sticking out his chest.

"Billy, I am the senior investigating officer in the disappearance and death of Kitty Morris. I understand you recognised her picture from my colleagues who visited you earlier?"

Billy shook his head and let out a deep sigh. "Yeah. Fucking tragic. What the fuck happened to her? I only saw her recently."

"That's what we're trying to find out. Did you know her well?"

"Not really. I knew of her. Said hello to her occasionally. She used to come in here to watch the boys playing on the machines. But I sometimes saw her outside hanging around with all the other kids."

Abby made a few notes whilst she studied the man. He was smartly dressed, in a white Fred Perry polo shirt, with tight trousers, which she noticed finished about two inches too short, to reveal suede moccasins with no socks. Clearly trendy in his eyes, but she begged to differ.

"You didn't see anything suspicious, any strangers talking to her, or see her getting into any bother?" Scott asked.

"Nah, give it a rest, give it a rest, mate," Billy fired back, glancing up at the ceiling. He threw a hand over his mouth, as if to stifle a laugh. It was an odd reaction. "As I said, I didn't really know her. I have my work cut out making sure the kids don't nick any of the drinks or sweets whilst they are in here. I haven't got much time to see what's happening out there," he said, nodding in the direction of outside.

"Who owns this place?" Scott asked.

"The boss, Duncan Prowse. He owns the joint."

"And is Duncan around?"

"Not at the moment. He pops in and out. He leaves me to it. He knows I can handle the place on my own," Billy replied with a degree of cockiness in his tone.

"Can you get Duncan to call us on this number?" Scott asked, slipping his business card across the counter.

"Sure... Sure."

Scott thanked him for his time before moving to the chip shop. Kristos, the owner, greeted him. Scott asked the same questions again. Kristos talked about his after-school trade, and how he was busiest between three thirty p.m. and five p.m., when the schoolkids from the nearby school dropped in.

Their conversation was drowned out occasionally by the

sound of an SDS drill ploughing through the brick wall that separated the chip shop from a small, narrow, empty shop next door.

"What's going on here?" Scott asked, looking in the direction of the building work.

Kristos laughed. "We are having building work done. There was a florist next door. Bloody tiny place. Anyway, their lease came to an end, so I snapped it up. I thought I'd knock through and create a little seating area there, have a little kitchen and storeroom, so we can offer a wider range of takeaway food."

"How long have your builders been here?"

"Just over a week now. They're a good bunch. Jakub is overseeing the work. He's very conscientious and a hard worker, but definitely quieter of the two. The other one is a bit of a live wire."

Kristos confirmed Kitty's picture looked familiar, although he commented there was usually dozens of children hanging around outside, so it was hard to be precise about how often he had seen her.

Scott and Abby thanked him and stepped into the building site. Arc lights lit the darkened space, highlighting dust particles floating in the air. Plasterboard, plaster bags and timber were propped up to one side; red bricks littered the floor, and the earthy smell of plaster dust lingered in the air.

Beyond the dusty environment, Scott tracked down the two builders doing the work. They introduced themselves as Dale Walsh and Jakub Nowak. Dale appeared to be the talkative one of the two. He dusted off his clothes and greeted them with a broad smile. Scott soon realised why. Jakub was

Polish and his command of English was limited to a few greetings.

"Have either of you seen this girl?" Scott asked the pair, holding up a picture of Kitty.

The men crowded in around the photo to get a better look. Jakub shook his head, offering nothing more than "no" in response.

Dale, on the other hand, was a lot more animated. "Yeah, I've seen her before. Cheeky little girl."

"You spoke to her?" Abby asked.

"Nah, not me," he replied, kicking dust around on the floor with his feet.

"But you said she was cheeky?"

Dale nodded in Abby's direction. "By that, I mean, I could hear her banter outside. She had a bit of a mouth on her. She was a bit flirty with the boys. She even whistled at me a few times when I was unloading stuff from the van."

"But you never spoke to her?" Abby pushed.

"Nope. She's jailbait. I'm not that stupid. I could go into town on a Friday or Saturday night and cop off with a bird my own age, no problems. You'd be a mug to go near any of those kids."

Scott gathered little more of significance before thanking them for their time and letting them return to work.

"What did you think of that?" Abby asked, as she followed Scott out into the street. "Cocky little fucker."

"Which one? Dale or Billy?"

Abby huffed. "Come to think of it, both."

"Well, everyone appears to have seen her the day before she disappeared. It all sounded fine, and there was no unusual activity and no one hanging around either. Kristos said there were at least thirty or more kids most afternoons. But that doesn't give us much to go on."

"Was it just me or did both Billy and Dale bother you?" Abby asked, as they walked back to the car.

"No, it wasn't just you. Billy spent far too much time repeating himself and staring up at the ceiling. That suggested to me he was either making up stuff or lying. And when he threw his hand over his mouth, that only made me more certain."

Abby had noticed that behaviour as well. They had both seen that in interviews when suspects were attempting to hide something from them.

With training in eye-accessing cues, Scott began to form the opinion that Billy was hiding something. Dale had also appeared to be less than truthful, as he'd spent more time kicking dust around with his feet than maintaining eye contact. Despite all of that, Scott was no nearer to getting the answers he sought.

In particular, he was still unable to account for the last twenty-four hours of Kitty's life.

13

I *always thought that trust must come before love but I disagree with that, because love and trust can come at the same time. It's so easy to buy it. It's so easy to make promises and break them.*

He laughed as he sat in his chair in contemplation.

The room filled with music from his phone again, a gentle nursery rhyme that played on repeat.

Mary, Mary, quite contrary,
how does your garden grow?
With silver bells, and cockle shells,
and pretty maids all in a row.

A tightening in his face replaced his smile. His eyes closed, as thoughts came flooding back to him. He had accepted humiliation as part of his early life. He had managed to keep a lid on it for so long until that day, when being the butt of all jokes had turned into him becoming the focus of their brutality and viciousness. A tear squeezed from the corner of his eye as he took in a deep breath. Slow and steady breaths were what he needed now.

When love and attention are given away immediately, with no conditions or explanations, the trust arrives too. Perhaps that is why people recommend caution or call it foolish, but to me it never is. Trusts are broken, lies are told. For us to believe in what we seek, we must know what it means to be what we don't want to be. Being sad makes you realise how valuable being happy is and how important revenge is. Being weak makes you know what it means to be strong, and I am strong now.

And there she was now, asleep, looking young and innocent.

Stupid bitch.

She was wearing the gift, looking so pleased to have it. It was a promise of things to come. To be regarded as a grownup and not a silly little child with a pathetic crush. How foolish she was.

But that was fine, because she was dreaming now, mumbling and talking to herself.

It wouldn't be long for her.

14

The rich, warming smells of pizza filled the air as the team gathered around the whiteboard. Scott had called ahead and ordered a large take out. Its arrival whipped everyone into a frenzy as they grabbed slices of pizza, potato wedges, and spicy chicken wings.

Mike appeared to be eating for two as he layered up his pizza slices to create a triple decker, which he heartedly tucked into, much to Helen's disgust. Pig and trough were a few of the words Helen levelled at Mike as she delicately picked on a corn cob. Mike didn't appear fazed in any way. He even opened his mouth mid-chew to show her his half-eaten pizza, just to annoy Helen further.

Scott asked them to quieten down when the conversation descended into insults. They were like a bunch of kids at a party.

"Mike, considering you started this, you can begin," Scott barked.

Mike grunted something incomprehensible before placing

his pizza down and wiping his mouth. "I've been running background checks on Kitty's parents. Nothing raised any red flags for me. Ellen Morris is thirty-nine and an office manager for an educational training company in Hove. She's been there for eleven years, and has had no run-ins or problems."

"And the dad?" Scott asked.

"Squeaky clean again. Alan Morris is forty-two years old, and a self-employed sparky. He's had no run-ins with the police, and his work record checks out. I took a look at his profile on checkatrade.com, and he's got a string of glowing testimonials from previous customers. Kitty was their only child. I also took the opportunity to speak to their neighbours, and they didn't flag anything either. They seemed like a nice family, and they made conversation with their neighbours."

"No domestics?"

Mike shrugged. "The odd shouting match, high-pitched yelling, but mainly between Kitty and her parents. Nothing violent, and no police attendances. They've lived at that current address for the past nineteen years, moving there to be in the catchment of the school."

Scott looked at the whiteboard and at Kitty's picture. Nothing suggested her possible suicide was connected with problems at home, which meant Scott needed to look for another motive.

Abby took a moment to update the rest of the team on their visit to Stop Out and the chip shop. She still found the name of the chip shop amusing, which caused her to laugh. But the amusement ended there as she continued, expressing her concern about Billy and Dale and whether they were being economical with the truth. Scott agreed both individuals needed to be investigated further and would probably need another chat.

"What can you tell us about your visit to Claudia's parents?" Scott asked Helen.

"Well, naturally, she's very upset and concerned. Claudia's been missing all day, and she is beside herself. Even though we've got officers combing the streets and chasing up her friends list, officers on the scene have found it difficult to keep Claudia's mum at home. She's been insistent on getting out there to look for her child."

"Any problems at home?"

"Nothing of significance, guv. I asked Emma, her mum, what Claudia was like, and she painted a picture of a strong and confident girl who spoke her mind. She said she could be a bit lippy and would go off the deep end if you had a go at her."

Scott tapped the end of his pen on the table, weighing up the information. "And did you get the impression there had been any disagreements recently between Claudia and her mum, which would have led to Claudia running off?"

"I didn't get that impression, guv. But then again, what we see in stressful times like this might not be a true reflection of the situations that preceded it. Emotions were running high when Raj and I turned up. She was screaming the place down, and the poor officers who were with her were getting the brunt of her attack. It took a while to calm her down before we got any sense out of her."

"That ties in with what we heard from the headmistress," Raj added. "She said Claudia liked to be the centre of attention and had a mouth to back it up. Claudia and Kitty were thick as thieves and a formidable pair when together in school."

Scott stood and walked up to the whiteboard. He tapped on Claudia's picture. "What concerns me is Claudia and Kitty were the best of friends. Kitty disappeared and appears to have taken her own life, possibly under the influence of something, which we'll know more about tomorrow when tox reports are back, and now her best friend has disappeared."

None of the officers said it but they were all thinking the same thing. Would Claudia end up the same way?

Scott felt like he was repeating himself as he handed out the tasking for the next day. The focus of attention needed to be around the shops. Kitty was last seen there, so it was highly likely Claudia may have been there as well, giving them a clue as to who had last seen or spoken to her. He also stressed the urgency in tracking down every shred of CCTV footage from the surrounding area. Kitty and Claudia must have been captured on footage somewhere. With the team still unable to explain what had happened in the last twenty-four-hours of Kitty's life, their task had now been complicated by her best friend's disappearance.

After sending the team home for the evening, Scott returned to his office and turned to his trusted pad of paper and pen. He had written Kitty's name on it, with other annotations relating to the school and the places she often visited. Claudia's name had been added, with salient points and interconnections. Both girls appeared to come from decent homes; they attended the same school, were in the same year group, and were best friends. They appeared to hang out socially, but that was where the trail ran cold.

He was interrupted from his thoughts when Abby appeared in his doorway. "Are you not going home?"

Scott rocked back in his chair and locked his hands

behind his head. "I am. I was trying to make sense of all of this. I'm sure there's more to this, but we haven't uncovered the right leads yet."

Abby rested her head on the door frame. "Sometimes when we look too hard, we confuse ourselves."

Scott smiled. "Don't get all philosophical on me." He shook his head and yawned. "I'm not even sure that philosophical was the right word. It just sounds good." He winked.

"Get yourself home. I'm sure you'd much rather be at home with Cara than here. The job gets enough of your time already."

"That's very true, Abby. Cara is on a conference call until about nine tonight. I'll probably go home and put my feet up in front of the telly and chill. How about you? Are you still happy with the way things are going?"

Abby rolled her eyes. She hoped they weren't going to have one of those *discussions* again.

"Don't look at me like that, Abby. I'm asking as your friend, not your boss. I care for you, and I want to make sure you're okay."

Abby offered a soft smile and stared at Scott. A brief silence lingered between them, a comfortable silence. "I'm fine. You don't need to worry about me. I'm a big girl. And in reply to your question, yes, things are still going well and I'm really happy with the situation. It's just my boss keeps annoying me by asking stupid questions." She threw him a smug grin.

Scott held his arms up. "I'm innocent. I am showing you my caring and compassionate side, and that doesn't come out too often, so don't knock it. But, before you have another go at me, get your arse out of here and go home to your kids. I'll see you in the morning."

"Yes, sir," Abby replied, giving him a military salute and turning on her heels.

Scott didn't move for the next few minutes, his eyes still fixed on the empty doorway where Abby had just stood. He couldn't describe his feelings but there were times when he wanted to give her a hug to reassure her that she was going to be okay. Maybe it was a kind of big brother, protection love. But whatever it was, he enjoyed being around her.

Scott took a deep breath to shake himself from his reverie. Though he wanted to go home, he had another idea. He grabbed his jacket and dashed out of the office, switching off the light as he left.

15

In the dark, the reflective strips from the police cars were trapped in his headlights as Scott drove into Clarke Avenue, the road where Claudia's family lived. Several police cars and officers on foot were cruising the surrounding area, looking for any sightings of her. She had been missing for twelve hours, and yet it was a fifteen-minute walk from her house to the school.

As Scott pulled up, he noticed several residents milling about the street, doing whatever they could to help the police presence, peering into front gardens, and shining their torches to illuminate their search.

A uniformed officer stood outside Claudia's house as Scott walked up the path. The officer acknowledged Scott, giving him a quick update. Their conversation was interrupted when a middle-aged woman raced out of her house with desperate hope in her eyes.

"Claudia, where's my Claudia? Have you found her?" she pleaded, her voice hoarse and broken.

Scott shook his head as he stepped into the hallway. He

ushered the woman into the front lounge, away from prying eyes. As he walked past the stairs, he saw a young boy sitting on the top step, worry lines and sadness etched in his features.

"I'm afraid not, Mrs White. I can assure you we've pulled in every available resource to look for her. I have officers scouring every street between here and her school. Every alleyway, front garden, back garden, garage, and lock-up is being checked for any signs of Claudia."

Claudia's dad, Frank, joined them. With cropped hair and a barrel chest, he looked a menacing figure, his heavily tattooed arms only reinforcing that image. He placed a protective arm around his wife. Scott expected the man to have a go at him, and complain they were not doing enough, but he did nothing of the sort. He looked at Scott through bloodshot eyes.

"Mr White, I was telling your wife that we're doing every-thing possible to find Claudia."

Frank only nodded.

Scott took a moment to look around the lounge. Family pictures lined the shelves of a bookcase. Some were of Claudia standing with her brother, the boy sitting at the top of the stairs. Others showed happier times, family photographs taken by the beach, and in restaurants, all sporting healthy tans.

"Has Claudia done anything like this before?" he asked Emma.

Emma shook her head. "Never. She's been late from school on the odd occasion – too busy having fun, I guess. But only by an hour or two."

"Is there anywhere she would have gone, to her friend's perhaps?" Scott asked.

"No. Nowhere. Why isn't she answering her phone?" Emma mumbled.

Scott didn't have an answer. He didn't have answers for any of the questions they were asking. "I understand you contacted her friends?"

Emma nodded. "When she didn't arrive at school I called all of them. Anyone I could think of. But of course, no one answered because they were all in school. They're not allowed to use their phones..." She trailed off as tears fell.

"Did you notice any changes in her behaviour in the last few days?"

Emma shrugged, lost in her own thoughts of despair. Scott wasn't sure she had heard his question. He took a step back when Claudia's parents embraced each other, seeking support and comfort from one another.

"Is it okay if I take a look around her room?" Scott asked softly.

Frank nodded. "Your officers have already done that."

"I know. But I also like to do it for myself."

Frank showed the way to Claudia's room before returning to comfort his wife.

As Scott made his way upstairs, Claudia's younger brother was nowhere to be seen. He walked past a closed bedroom door, which he assumed belonged to the brother, as the other two doors were wide open. He found Claudia's bedroom and flipped on the light before allowing his eyes to travel round the room. He snapped on a pair of latex gloves.

This space wasn't too dissimilar from Kitty's. A typical girl's bedroom with lilac patterned wallpaper, a dressing table overflowing with hairbrushes, makeup, sprays and perfumes, and an array of clothes scattered in piles around the floor. A heap of shoes was wedged into one corner of the bedroom.

A large TV hung from the wall opposite her bed, with fairy lights taped all around it, looking as if Claudia had forgotten to take down her Christmas decorations.

Scott spent a few moments searching through her wardrobes, looking under piles of clothes for anything that might be hidden. He moved over to her bed and searched under the mattress, and then under the bed frame. There was nothing but dust where the bed hadn't been moved for months for a proper clean. A small bedside cabinet with a little lamp proved a useful perch for empty bottles of Tango and discarded sweet wrappers. There were so many similarities between this room and Kitty's. He remembered as a boy he'd kept his room spotless. He would make his bed every morning. And every Sunday he would vacuum it, and get out the duster and a can of Mr Sheen to tackle every surface in his room. How times had changed.

He pulled open the drawer to find even more discarded sweet wrappers, pens, an old broken phone with a cracked screen, and several pairs of wired headphones, their leads tangled into a ball of confusion. But it wasn't the mess which caught his attention.

He paused for a second as fear spread through his body. He picked up a small, clear plastic bag with brown tablets, and held it up to the light. A crown emblem had been stamped into each tablet. Farther back in the drawer, he found the remnants of a half-rolled-up joint. He placed them both in separate, clear evidence bags and made his way downstairs.

"Mr and Mrs White, have you ever seen these before?"

Scott asked, presenting both bags to them. Their eyes widened, their lips parted in shock.

Frank spoke first. "I've never seen them. Where were they?"

"I found them tucked into the drawer of her bedside cabinet."

Emma shook her head in disbelief. "They're not Claudia's. They can't be Claudia's. We've spoken to her so many times about not taking drugs, and the dangers of taking things like that," she said, jabbing a finger at the bags. "Maybe she was looking after them for someone."

Scott wanted that to be true, but his intuition was telling him something else.

16

Scott raced into the office ahead of the rest of his team, keen to make an early start. The truth was he was desperate for news on Claudia's disappearance. He knew not to expect much as he made his way through the building. The night shift had been out until the early hours accompanying uniformed colleagues in their search for the girl, and his phone hadn't rung all night.

As every hour slipped by, the chances of finding her alive diminished. He had struggled to sleep, waking every few hours and checking his phone, in case he had accidentally put it on silent. To avoid waking Cara, he had gone down in the early hours of the morning and settled on the sofa, slipping between periods of wakefulness and light sleep. An uncomfortable feeling gnawed at him that this wasn't going to end well.

He checked in with the night shift and, as expected, there had been no sightings or word of Claudia. Her parents had declined the help of the family liaison officer, even as they struggled to hang on to their sanity.

Scott stood in CID's kitchen stirring his coffee, lost in deep thought. Dozens of bits of information had been catalogued in his brain, and his mind was busily sifting through it like a complex puzzle. None of the pieces were making sense, no clues were forming.

Why did Kitty do it? What drove her to do something so extreme? Where is Claudia?

He took his coffee back to his office and called through to the forensics department before making his way down to find Matt. There, he found him sifting through reams of paperwork from the labs overnight.

"Morning, Matt. How're you?"

"Don't ask. I reckon dodgy chicken in a curry last night. It played havoc with my insides and I hardly slept. I still don't feel right this morning," Matt replied, rubbing his head, and stretching out a yawn.

"I know the feeling. But in my case, I didn't eat a dodgy ruby." Scott pulled out the two small, clear evidence bags from Claudia's room and dropped them onto Matt's desk.

"What are these?" Matt asked, leaning across the desk and examining the packages.

"We've got another girl missing, Claudia White. She is Kitty's friend. I found these in one of her bedroom drawers last night. It doesn't take a genius to figure out what the joint is, but I've not seen brown tablets like that before. What do you make of them?"

Matt let out a long breath, saying, "Well, I agree with you on the joint. That's more than likely cannabis. As for the tablets... we'll need to get them analysed to be certain. But I think your day is about to get a lot worse." Matt searched through several toxicology reports. "Ah, here it is."

He mumbled to himself as he read the words aloud, then he passed the report to Scott.

"Kitty had traces of LSD in her blood. *Lysergic acid diethylamide* is the correct name," Matt explained.

"A powerful hallucinogenic drug." Scott shook his head. "I've not come across it much in my cases."

"As you probably know, it often comes as small squares of paper with pictures on them, known as tabs or blotters. LSD can also be sold as a liquid, or as tiny pellets or pills known as microdots. If consumed as a liquid, LSD has no taste at all. LSD tabs on the other hand taste like the paper."

Scott skimmed through the notes. He looked up at Matt. "What effect does it have on kids?"

Matt shrugged. "It depends on the person. Generally, it gives people an intense 'trip' where everything seems distorted around them. The colours, sounds, even objects can all appear strange, and some have an out-of-body experience."

Scott was shocked to learn Kitty had been using this.

Matt continued. "I'm telling you what you already know, but a user can often see and hear things that aren't actually there as they start to hallucinate. Everything becomes distorted. It can feel like time, or even movement is speeding up or slowing down, and users can begin to experience double vision. It's a pretty potent substance and its unpredictability is the most worrying thing in any situation." Matt referred to extra information on his computer before continuing. "Some users may feel like they are going through a near-death experience or go through an intense period of quiet and internal reflections."

"How long does this stuff last in kids, Matt? Is it like a

quick trip or can the user experience these reactions for hours?"

"Your guess is as good as mine. A lot of it depends on the size of the person, their body weight, whether they've eaten anything recently, or even if they're taking any other substances in conjunction. According to the database the experiences are intense and short, perhaps only lasting minutes, and less than a few hours."

"But surely if Kitty had been taking this on a regular basis, or even occasionally, others around her would have noticed these reactions? Her friends, or even her family?" Scott suggested.

"You would think so, mate. It leads me to think that this was a very recent thing in her life, if not her first experience. If Kitty was sitting there with her heart racing and her pupils dilated, whilst displaying erratic behaviour, someone would have picked up on it. The after-effects are just as bad, with flashbacks of the experience, anxiety, and paranoia. The effects on an adult are pretty extreme and varied. No two people go through the same experience. In a child, it's a different outcome altogether. They have smaller bodies, organs that are still developing, and their bodies can't tolerate what an adult can. A small amount could lead to an adverse reaction and a night in hospital for obs. A large, deliberate dose could be catastrophic."

"This doesn't make sense, Matt. We've had no indicators to suggest she took drugs, but Claudia is a different matter," Scott said, nodding at the substances he'd found in Claudia's bedroom.

"LSD is not the run-of-the-mill drugs we usually see in Brighton. The drug was originally used by the CIA and the military in mind control experiments, designed to produce robotic assassins with no will of their own. That may seem like a bizarre idea, Scott, but the reality-warping capacities of LSD are powerful enough to turn even the sharpest mind into a blank slate, into someone incapable of preserving their self-control or autonomy."

Scott stood open-mouthed as he listened to Matt's history lesson. *The military. The CIA.*

Matt continued. "Then, of course, it became a popular recreational drug in the sixties with Woodstock, the summer of love, and all that kind of stuff. LSD works by disrupting the natural operation of serotonin, an important neurotransmitter involved in behaviour, sensory perception, and the functioning of the autonomic nervous system. All of these are still evolving in kids, so the effects in them are diverse and far-reaching."

Scott nodded. Kitty would have suffered.

Matt added. "Any drug can kill if enough is ingested. It's so random. Doctors can't say for certain what happens when people take more than the usual dose."

Scott scrubbed a hand down his face. "That's what worries me, Matt. If Kitty got easy access to LSD, who's going to be next?"

17

Random theories raced through Scott's mind as he stared at his computer screen. The fear looped around until there was no room for anything else. The tox reports showing LSD in Kitty's system threw the investigation in a different direction. What worried Scott the most was how she had come into possession of such a powerful drug.

Scott Googled LSD. He spent the next hour trawling through the information. Much of what he read he knew; the rest had been covered by Matt. Articles detailed how users reported being taken to other realms, speaking to divine beings, and were convinced of life after death.

"A deep state of peace and happiness where users are launched into other dimensions," Scott read aloud. Another article discussed how LSD differed from other hallucinogenic drugs. "LSD takes you to a place completely different from this world, as opposed to other drugs that only modify your relationship with the one you already exist in."

According to this article, the effects were so intense and abstract, it was hard for users to explain their "trip".

Scott stumbled upon a piece of research which suggested the effects of LSD generally concluded within thirty to forty minutes of taking it, but the next bit he read sent an icy-cold shiver through him and made the hairs on the back of his neck stand up.

The article mentioned volunteers who had agreed to take part in research studies. These volunteers had experienced the classic, near-death experience that confirmed their beliefs of it and made them feel good about the prospect of dying. Scott wasn't sure he agreed with the last part. The article then highlighted how, in an altered state of mind, volunteers would experience a state of nirvana where everything felt chilled and distorted – unless it was a "bad trip". Then they were left in a state of panic, confusion, or sadness.

Footage from the bus showing Kitty's final moments replayed in his mind as he scanned further search results. Many carried the same interpretations of LSD, and further research studies threw up identical results.

Scott pushed back his chair and stood, his mind processing what this meant for Kitty, as he made his way to the kitchen. Random theories and thoughts crammed his mind to such an extent, they drowned out all sounds around him, including Abby, who had just arrived and was putting her lunch away in the fridge.

"Earth calling Scott, hello?"

"Shit, sorry, Abby. I was miles away."

"The day has only started and you already looked stressed."

Scott washed his spoon and left it on the draining board.

"According to Matt's tox reports, Kitty was under the influence of LSD."

The news clearly surprised Abby. Her eyes widened.

"Exactly, that was my first reaction," Scott added before revealing what Matt had told him, and what he had discovered online this morning. "Kitty would have been so off her face that I doubt she would have known what she was doing."

Abby followed Scott back to the CID floor and the whiteboard at the end of the room. He grabbed a red marker and in big letters wrote "LSD" next to Kitty's photo.

"The tox reports came back overnight and there were traces of LSD in the samples analysed," Scott began. "Considering how powerful a drug it is and how young she was, she must have been completely out of her mind. I bet she had no idea what she was doing when she climbed on that viaduct. LSD also affects judgement and behaviour. A young or inexperienced user can often find themselves in dangerous situations."

"Shit. Where the fuck did she get that stuff from around here?" Abby fumed.

"That's what we need to find out. Firstly, who's dealing it, and secondly, who's supplying it to underage kids. It's starting to make sense." Scott tapped Kitty's picture. "It explains both the dashcam footage and the on-board footage from the bus. Kitty didn't scream or show any signs of distress, nor did she appear to panic when she was standing on the ledge. She appeared calm and relaxed. Do you remember how she had her arms outstretched? She was looking up towards the sky. She was in the throes of a bloody hallucination."

"And that's why she stepped off the ledge so effortless-ly..." Abby sighed.

"Abby, can you do me a favour and get in touch with Kitty's school this morning? Find out if there've been any issues with drugs amongst the student population. She may have been offered LSD at school, and if so, there could be other kids walking around with this stuff in their pockets. The last thing we need is another tragedy."

THE COLOURS SWIRLED around her like the inside of a kaleidoscope. Her cheeks ached from smiling too much, but she didn't care. She wanted everyone to experience this happiness, this joy, this journey. People called her name, telling her to experience a life beyond her existence, to journey to a place where only happiness and love existed. Their voices came from the sky. To others, it probably looked like a thick and dark grey blanket of cloud above, but to her it was pure blue brilliance. With the sun set so high in the sky, its warmth bathed her face.

She staggered a little as she glanced down, fascinated by the lines running between the pavement slabs. Her eyes were wide, staring into the distance one minute then at the ground the next. Everything appeared so hazy and soft. She loved how everything appeared in pairs.

Sweat poured from her brow, and her heart thumped loudly in her chest, but neither bothered her. This was the best journey she had ever been on. She flapped her arms whimsically by her side and twirled on the spot, her restless-ness urging her to keep moving.

For a moment she closed her eyes, and all she saw were

lots of books opening, with colourful rainbows and shooting stars erupting from them. Upon opening her eyes, it felt different, like her surroundings were closing in on her. People were crowding her space, walking by, staring at her, and yet she couldn't see their faces.

Alarm bells should have been ringing in those who walked by, especially because of her outfit. A girl in school uniform, staggering and swaying, her eyes rolling back in her head. There should have been concern on their faces. Someone should have stopped to ask if she was okay, but they ignored her.

Somewhere off in her consciousness, a big box floated towards her. She smiled, knowing it was coming to meet her. She stepped off the pavement.

The sound of a horn blaring and the screech of brakes stopped time. People froze on the spot, shock and panic contorting their features.

A pause. A heartbeat.

Then the screams started.

18

Scott had barely made it halfway to Meadows's office to update him before Abby came running down the corridor, a look of panic on her face.

"Guv... guv, hold up."

Scott spun round and looked at her in surprise. "What's the matter?"

"Reports are coming in of a pedestrian being struck by a bus in Elm Grove. It's a fatality."

"Uniform can deal with that unless there is anything suspicious."

Abby shook her head. "I think this is one for us. A teenage girl stepped out in front of a bus. It looks like she died on impact."

"Do officers at the scene have an identity?"

Abby closed her eyes and sighed. "Not yet. From what I gather, she's under the bus."

COLD TENTACLES of dread prickled Scott's skin as he entered Elm Grove. Child fatalities were becoming an all-too-regular occurrence for him as he attended the scene of a tragic accident for the second time in less than a week. The true extent of the incident became clear as Scott and Abby covered the last few yards on foot, having parked close to the outside cordon. Uniformed officers were keeping spectators and pedestrians one hundred metres away from the scene.

They checked in with the scene guard and added their signatures to the scene log before kitting up in paper suits and booties. The pair dipped under the inner cordon tape and made their way towards a double-decker bus which blocked the road.

"I'm already dreading this, guv." Abby groaned.

"If it makes you feel any better, so am I."

The fire service had erected a blue tarpaulin screen around the front of the bus, and a fleet of ambulances were treating shocked witnesses. Traffic officers congregated in the road, holding clipboards and cameras, as they conferred around the front of the bus. Several other officers stood on the opposite pavement, deep in discussion.

Scott's stomach flipped over at the sight before him.

Carnage. Again.

Sand scattered on the pavement in front of the bus had soaked up the blood that had trickled out from beneath it. Despite it being the morning and just after rush hour, Elm Grove had fallen into an eerie silence. A respectful silence, in Scott's opinion, as emergency services went about their work. The uniformed officer coordinating the scene picked out Scott as he approached, and headed towards him.

"Sir, Sergeant Appleby. I'm the scene coordinator for the

traffic division. I've arranged diversions at both ends of the street, and we are waiting for more resources."

"Thank you, sergeant. What have we got?" Scott asked, as he stood close to the temporary screen.

"We're still getting witness statements, but from what we have managed to gather so far, a schoolgirl was acting erratically, and then without warning, she stepped out in front of the bus. Since it happened only a few feet in front of the bus, the driver didn't stand a chance at stopping."

"You said erratically?" Scott asked.

"Yes, sir. A few eyewitnesses commented the girl was staggering around on the pavement, as if drunk." The sergeant screwed up his face, as if even saying the words sounded odd to him. "She was flapping her arms by her side and smiling at everyone who walked past, but her eyelids were drooping, as if she was intoxicated."

"Okay, sergeant, let's take a look," Scott announced, taking a deep breath to ready himself.

Scott nodded for Abby to follow the sergeant first. She widened her eyes in reply and mouthed, "Why me? You're the boss. You go first."

They exchanged a few silent messages until Scott shrugged his shoulders and disappeared behind the tarpaulin, followed a few seconds later by Abby.

A scattered blood pattern spread from the lower section of the bus up to the windscreen. From somewhere beneath the giant vehicle, a trickle of blood matter snaked downhill. The fire service had temporarily covered the worst of it with sand before retreating and waiting for additional resources.

From where they stood they could see little. The current scene matched the early reports. The girl had been dragged so deep under the bus there was no visible sign of her.

"How far did she go under?" Scott asked.

"She is about halfway under the bus. It took longer for the driver to stop the bus because it was already going downhill. Poor cow," the sergeant replied.

"Okay, make sure all witness statements are on the system and copies are sent to us as a matter of urgency. I also want the on-board camera footage as soon as possible," Scott said, pointing at the cab.

He walked around to the side of the bus.

About halfway, he gritted his teeth and got down on his hands and knees. He took a deep breath before peering under the bus. His stomach clenched into a ball of emotion. At first, it looked like nothing more than a rolled-up pile of clothes, but to the left, he saw the mangled remains of a pair of legs. He fired up the light on his phone and shone it into the darkened space, before instantly regretting it and turning away.

Scott composed himself before standing and joining Abby and the sergeant, who stood a few feet away.

"How are we going to get her out?" he asked.

"We are waiting for a couple of specialist recovery vehicles," the sergeant said. "We can't move the bus backwards or forwards without disturbing the body. We're going to have one recovery truck towards the rear of the bus. It will secure the bus in place, so it doesn't roll farther down the hill. We will have a second recovery truck positioned to the front, and they'll use their winch to lift the front of the bus off the ground. They'll then place blocks and hydraulic jacks beneath the bus to allow the fire service to recover the body safely."

"Do we know who she is?" Abby asked but guessed the victim's identity.

"Not at the moment, skip. But it looks like the victim was a pupil at Causeway secondary school. I've got friends who have a son and daughter at that school, and I would recognise their uniform from a mile away."

The sergeant confirmed Abby's suspicions. The victim was probably Claudia White.

Scott glanced at Abby who looked visibly upset. There was no sign of the grey Superdry rucksack that Emma White said her daughter took to school every day, and though he couldn't be certain that it was Claudia yet, he was able to make out the victim wore shiny, black Prada shoes, and amongst the pile of tangled clothes, a Louis Vuitton scarf was clearly visible, both of which Claudia wore to school every day.

"Where's the driver?" Scott asked.

"He's in the ambulance over there, sir. David Cribbs," the sergeant replied, flicking his gaze in that direction. A middle-aged man under several blankets glanced up as Scott approached. His body was trembling. His eyes were wide, and dark as black buttons.

Scott noticed the cold, soulless stare. It was as if he'd experienced a ghostly aberration and couldn't process it. He looked broken and numb.

"I'm Detective Inspector Baker," Scott began, flashing his ID before taking a seat opposite. "How are you holding up, David?"

Cribbs stared through Scott, grief moistening his eyes.

Scott let out a slow breath. He couldn't even imagine what the man must be feeling. "They'll be taking you to hospital shortly to check you over. You've been through a traumatic shock, and I'm sorry for that, but I wondered if you could tell me what happened, David?"

The driver said nothing for a few minutes. Scott held back from saying anything too, giving him space to process the confusion that engulfed him.

"David?" Scott prompted.

"Um... um. I don't know," David replied, shaking his head in consternation.

Scott prompted him. "You were driving down Elm Grove then your bus collided with a pedestrian. Do you remember that?"

David's lips moved, muttering words. His narrowed eyes darted back and forth. "Yes, I remember... The girl. Oh, my God!"

Nodding encouragement, Scott leant forward. "What can you remember seeing?"

Cribbs screwed up his face, licking his bottom lip as it wobbled uncontrollably.

The recollections would be challenging but Scott needed more. "Can you remember anything before the moment of impact?"

David raised a shoulder slowly, as if doubting his own thoughts. He thrust his hands out. "One minute the road was clear then she was there. In front of me, staring at me through the windscreen." A shiver of fear pulsed through the man, causing his body to shudder. "The sound. Thud. She disappeared." His words jumped and quivered in time with his lips.

Scott thanked the driver and exited the ambulance.

"Smiling..." David added.

That single word stopped him in his tracks. His stomach clenched.

Scott turned round. "Sorry?"

"She... was... smiling," David mumbled again, falling forward in a heap.

"How was he?" Abby asked as she joined Scott.

"Pretty fucked up, understandably. Abby, arrange for an officer to accompany the driver to the hospital. Let's see if we can get him interviewed once he's been assessed. He might not be in a fit state for a while but it's worth a try."

"Agreed," Abby confirmed, as she stared at the flurry of activity around the bus.

"It's going to take ages to recover the body. It would be a job and a half on a flat road, but the fact it's on a thirty-degree incline makes this a bloody nightmare," Scott said to no one in particular.

"What about Cara?" Abby asked.

"We don't need to call her at the moment. There's nothing for her to see, or access for that matter. And right now, I need to go and see Claudia's parents."

19

Scott stood on the pavement facing Claudia's house. A family home once filled with laughter was now cloaked in a painful emptiness.

Shit, he hated this part of the job the most. He always felt their pain and despair. Their sadness poured through him. It flooded through every cell of his being. Just a few hours ago there had been hope. A tiny flicker which had kept the family's spirits up, a glimmer of a promise that Claudia would finally return home to be wrapped in a warm and loving embrace by her parents.

Now, it looked like a reckless drug dealer had stolen that chance away. There was nothing Scott could say or do to dampen the pain and anguish of these distraught parents. He knew their despair would sit heavy like concrete in their veins. He looked at his shoes, steadying himself before he strode up the path.

As he approached, he saw Emma White jump up from her seat in the lounge. She ran to the window, her heavy, black gaze boring into Scott, searching for any sign that she hadn't hoped in vain. Though he kept poker-faced, her face creased with despair. A small shake of her head turned into a violent swaying as she raced from the lounge window, through the hall and to the front door. She pulled it open with a force that sent it crashing into the wall.

"Where is she...? Where is my girl?" Emma screamed, her voice a painful screech that tore from her throat and alerted all her neighbours.

She hammered her fists on Scott's chest, pleading for news.

"Mrs White, a child has been involved in a fatal accident. We can't be certain of the child's identity at the moment, but I thought you should know, it may be Claudia."

The news punctured her reality with such force, Emma's knees buckled. Scott caught her before she fell and wrapped his arms around her waist. Her husband raced out into the hallway to help. Tears streaked his face.

She screamed, traumatised by the news. The wracking sobs shook her body in such a way, Scott couldn't bear it. Scott tried to console her as Emma's husband pulled his wife to his chest. A draw of breath interrupted her screaming sobs, so primal, it was as if her brain was being shredded from the inside.

The cry was so raw that Scott's eyes were soon wet with tears.

"But... but you can't be certain it's our Claudia?" Frank asked, as he sniffed away the snot.

Scott shook his head. "We can't be certain, but the victim *was* wearing a Causeway secondary school uniform, and we have no other reported cases of children missing from the school, or unauthorised absences. The victim also had a scarf and shoes matching the description Emma gave us."

"What happened?"

"We are not a hundred per cent sure at the moment. We've got officers at the scene doing a detailed investigation, but the child was hit by a bus, and sadly died at the scene." Scott kept the details brief, not wishing to reveal too much, and sparing her parents the added pain.

Frank hugged Emma tighter as she sobbed into his chest.

"But you can't be certain it's our Claudia?" Frank asked again.

Scott understood the need for her parents to hang onto any thread of hope to keep their world from imploding. It was difficult news for every parent to accept and come to terms with, and Claudia's parents were no different. His offer of extra police help in the form of a family liaison officer was declined, with Frank insisting they would deal with this on their own.

Frank walked his wife into the lounge where she curled up into a ball on the sofa and cried. He stifled his own cries to stay strong for his wife.

Scott left not long after with the promise he would update them when he had further information. The child would need to be formally identified, a task he was neither looking forward to nor wanting to put Frank and Emma through. Much depended on the state of the body once it was removed from under the bus. When that would happen he was unsure.

The longer it took, the harder it would be for Claudia's parents.

20

Meadows paced around his office as Scott relayed the details of the incident in Elm Grove, and his subsequent visit to Claudia's parents.

"This isn't great news for us, the school or parents in general," Meadows commented, rubbing his chin and pondering the fallout.

The local press had already been on the phone that morning seeking a response from the press team, and local TV crews had descended on Elm Grove, giving live updates as the recovery process continued. Reporters had stopped and dramatically questioned passers-by, gauging and looking for reactions. The more animated and shocked the response the better viewing figures for the TV channel.

Scott updated Meadows on the line of investigation that his team had followed, as well as news of the LSD found in Kitty's body, and the discovery of potentially illegal substances in Claudia's bedroom.

"Two best friends both died within a week in very extreme circumstances. Have you considered the possibility of a double-suicide pact?" Meadows speculated.

Scott nodded. "I did with Kitty to begin with, sir, but with the discovery of an illegal substance in her body, it added a different dimension to our work. And, if it had been a double-suicide pact, the chances are they would have taken their lives at the same time. The witness statement from the bus driver didn't suggest it was suicide. From his account, Claudia was smiling when she stepped off the kerb."

"Keep me updated on your progress today. We need to keep a tight control over what we're doing, and I'll speak to the press office. We can put out a response which will buy us time."

Meadows sat down and continued with his paperwork, signalling the meeting had ended.

———

THE TEAM GATHERED around the whiteboard. A picture of Claudia had the word "deceased" written beneath it.

"Right, team," Scott began, "we have another suspicious death, and we need to get answers quickly. Unfortunately, there's not much left of the victim, but the mortuary team will prep her body so her father can identify her in the next few hours. For the time being, we are going to assume it's Claudia White."

"This is bloody appalling," Mike commented. "I don't get it. From what we've seen on the bodycam footage, these two girls took their own lives in an extreme way."

"You're not wrong there, and what we need to do now is find out why. I know it feels like we've gone over all of this already, but we need to uncover everything we can about Claudia White. Go back over social media profiles, friendship circles, which we know Kitty was a large part of, and anything else we can uncover from the school, boyfriends, phone records – the whole lot."

"Her bag wasn't discovered at the scene, and my guess is her phone was either on her person or in her bag," Abby said. "Without both, we're running blind on who her recent contacts were."

Scott agreed and knew that for the time being they could work around that. "There's plenty more we need to discover first. What does concern me are the drugs I discovered in Claudia's bedroom. The fact Kitty had LSD in her body means we have one solid line of enquiry now and a connection between the pair of them. We have to focus on who is supplying LSD and whether they obtained it in or out of school."

A uniformed officer came through the double doors to the CID floor as Scott was in mid-flow, with a memory stick in hand. He handed it to Scott, informing him it was on-board footage from the bus involved that morning.

Scott passed it to Mike, who connected it to a laptop close by. They all crowded around the screen.

It showed a dual feed, with a front-facing camera capturing the road ahead as the bus travelled down Elm Grove towards Lewes Road. A second internal camera captured footage of the driver in his cab. Conditions on the road were good, traffic was light, the road was dry, so braking distances wouldn't have been extended. It was single-lane traffic in both directions, with a few small areas sectioned off for parking.

They watched for a few minutes as the bus weaved in

and out of the central islands and parked cars. The way the camera footage juddered suggested the driver was applying his brakes intermittently all the way down Elm Grove, to regulate his speed.

Nothing in the footage suggested a catastrophic event about to take place. As the bus continued its journey, from the left side of the driver's view and when the bus was no more than six to eight feet away, a small figure stepped out. Abby shuddered at the impact point, and the heavy thud which followed. It all happened so quickly that Mike had to rewind the short segment of clip and play it at half speed.

As Mike froze the tape, Claudia's face came into view, confirming their worst fears. She stepped into the road and collided with the bus in the space of a few seconds. The on-board audio from the bus captured the moment when the bus driver yelled, "Fuck!" The footage lurched as the driver slammed on his brakes. The bus travelled at least another twenty to thirty feet before it screeched to a halt. The on-board digital media also captured the sound of screams as passengers were thrown forward in their seats and the driver's utter shock as he shouted, "Shit, shit, shit!".

Sheer panic followed as the driver sat there in shock, unable to move or utter any further words. From somewhere within the bus the screams continued.

The CID team sat in silence, unable to comprehend what they had just witnessed. What concerned Scott were the remarkable similarities between the last few moments in both Kitty's life and Claudia's. He rewound the footage and paused it as Claudia's face came into view.

"Look at that. Claudia's smiling. Can you see what she's doing?"

Claudia had her arms outstretched in the same way Kitty had whilst she'd stood on the ledge of the viaduct.

Raj tutted in despair. "What I can't get over is why Claudia's smiling as she walks into the path of the bus. Anyone would think she wanted to hug it."

"I would say she was under the influence of LSD as well. That corroborates witness statements," Scott said. "We've got two best friends who both go to the same school, who have both died. One died in suspicious circumstances while under the influence of an illegal substance. Kitty had LSD in her system, and I bet you any money when we run a tox report on Claudia, she'll have the same substance in her bloodstream. Where in the hell are they getting it from?"

Scott instructed the team to double their efforts to speak to pupils at the school as well as local residents on the route from Claudia's home to the school. She'd disappeared somewhere along that journey, and it was vital for them to uncover her movements in the twenty-four-hour period between the disappearance and the discovery of her body that morning. He left it with Raj and Helen to organise a team of officers to begin large-scale questioning of pupils in Kitty and Claudia's year group. Scott confirmed he would join them when he could.

"Mike, I know you've spoken to the dealers already but target them again," Scott reiterated, jabbing his index finger on the whiteboard. "Someone has been dealing LSD, and somewhere along the chain, it has come into the girl's possession. It's not a common street drug and these teenage girls don't have a lot of money. Find the scrote doing this."

Mike stiffened. "I'll get onto it right away. I might have to knock a few heads together if I don't get a lot of cooperation."

"I didn't hear that, Mike, but I'll leave it to *your* judgement."

SCOTT AND ABBY spent the next few hours visiting both sets of parents. Kitty's parents, still coming to terms with the loss of their daughter, had questions for Scott, many of which he was unable to answer. The question her parents kept returning to was, "Why?"

He reassured them the investigation was still in its early stages, and that his team were fully committed to uncovering anything that would lead them to discover why Kitty had ended her life in such a tragic way.

It was an uneasy subject to broach but Scott relayed information about the LSD that had been found in Kitty's body. Ellen refused to believe her daughter would be involved in drugs. It wasn't something she knew much about, but she never imagined for one minute that her daughter would experiment with drugs. Scott knew many parents didn't fully understand what their children were up to. Social media, peer pressure, and lifestyle changes meant the children of this generation were growing up in a very different way to how their parents had. Sadly, parents like Kitty's still didn't fully understand the effects from the cultural shift.

Their visit to Claudia's parents had been challenging because it had been so recent. As they arrived, they saw floral tributes had been laid in the front garden from well-wishers and family. Several small teddies were dotted amongst the flowers, and messages attached to the tributes remembered Claudia in loving ways.

Scott had the unenviable task of confirming with the parents that footage taken from the bus had identified their daughter as the fatality. It was an inevitable conclusion that neither of her parents wanted to believe. The clear video footage now spared Claudia's dad from the difficult task of identifying his daughter's mangled remains.

Emma White had cried herself to sleep for a few hours before waking, looking exhausted and gaunt. Her eyes, lips, and cheeks were still puffy, red, and sore. Upon hearing the news, Frank, Claudia's dad, shifted from feeling broken and distraught, to anger. The subject of illegal substances being discovered in Claudia's bedroom only infuriated him further. Frank demanded the name of who had supplied those drugs to his daughter.

Scott diplomatically suggested that wouldn't be a wise move, reassuring Frank that his anger and frustration were understandable, but his threats to head up to the school and walk the corridors until he found the person who had given her the drugs would do little to help their investigation, or his grief. Frank angrily disagreed, his heavily tattooed arms flexing and stiffening as he punched the lounge door.

Rubbing his knuckles, Frank screamed, "If you don't find this bastard and soon, I will!"

Abby stepped in, attempting to calm the man. "Mr White, I understand your frustration. Feeling angry or vengeful, it's to be expected, but outbursts won't help your wife or Claudia's little brother. He needs his parents more than anything at this difficult time."

"Yeah, but it would make it a lot better knowing someone else was feeling what we are!"

"Please..." Abby said, her voice a soft plea.

Frank glared at Abby, the sinews of muscles in his cheeks flexing. He nodded before sinking into the sofa.

With their anguish weighing heavy on their hearts, Scott and Abby left Claudia's parents, with a promise to return as soon as they had more information.

21

F eeling tired and hungry, Scott dropped Abby at the station before heading off to meet Cara for a quick bite to eat. The thought of sitting in a restaurant and waiting to be served, and then waiting even longer for the food to arrive hadn't appealed to either of them.

Rather than meet in town, they had agreed to a place closer to home. Cara had chosen Wolfies in Hove for a quick fish and chip supper. With Wolfies being recognised as one of the best fish and chip shops in Brighton and Hove, it was the perfect place to stop for hot and scrumptious food.

Cara waited patiently outside, stomping her feet to keep the chill at bay, and glancing up and down the street for any sign of Scott. Within a few minutes, he was running down the road, shaking his head and silently mouthing "sorry" as he approached.

"Sorry, so sorry. I was running late and then I couldn't find parking... Typical," Scott said apologetically. He kissed Cara on the cheek.

"It's okay. I know you've been rushed off your feet today."

"That obvious, is it?" Scott replied, catching his breath as he opened the door. The instant aroma so familiar in every chip shop up and down the land assaulted their nostrils and made Scott's stomach grumble.

"Um, yeah. No text messages, no calls to tell me that you love me, both sure signs you were busy."

"Guilty as charged," Scott replied, holding up his hands in admission.

After they ordered two cod and chips, they grabbed a table close to the window and settled in. The headlights from passing cars lit up the darkened street, their beams reflecting off the parked cars on either side of the road.

They were ravenous by the time the food arrived. The smell of freshly battered fish and chunky chips fired up their taste buds. Their conversation ground to a halt while they liberally sprinkled salt and vinegar over their food. Then they savoured the first few mouthfuls.

"This... is... so good," Cara moaned, her eyes rolling, savouring the warm, soft flakes of cod, and the crunchiness of the batter.

"Tell me about it. I've hardly eaten all day. I'm not even sure it's going to be enough for me," Scott said between large mouthfuls.

Cara wiped her mouth and took a sip of her Dr Pepper before rubbing Scott's leg. "You really need to take better care of yourself. You're getting more and more tired these days, and you're definitely not eating enough. Maybe I need to do the old-fashioned thing and send you off to work with a packed lunch. I'm sure that would go down well with the team," she said, laughing.

"It's been a bit hectic. Abby and I saw both set of parents

this evening. I really do feel sorry for them. I wish we could get to the bottom of this case quicker."

"You will, Scottie. These things take time, which you and I both know, but sadly many parents in this situation want instant answers. They feel like knowing the truth will chase some of their agony away. And I know you want to do right by them. That's the kind of bloke you are. You're always worrying about other people's feelings."

Scott shrugged. "I guess. We haven't got much to go on at the moment other than the fact Kitty had LSD in her analysis, and my guess is Claudia will as well. That has to be the main thrust of our investigation."

"On the LSD front, we'll be sending away samples taken from Claudia's remains tomorrow, after we do the post-mortem. If it comes back positive, then that's sad but encouraging news?" Cara questioned.

Scott agreed, but it wasn't enough for him. Chasing down the supplier of LSD wasn't going to be easy. What he really needed was key sightings of both victims, and despite asking dozens of residents and scanning hours of CCTV footage, neither girl had been picked up on any recordings outside of school on the days of their disappearances.

Cara paused for a moment, her eyes wandering around the shop, as a few other diners tucked into their suppers as well. A young couple were at another table. They pulled their stools closer together so their legs were interlinked, and they shared smiles and laughs in between their mouthfuls. Cara's mouth curled up as she watched their playfulness. It was nice to see other couples sharing the closeness she enjoyed with her man.

Cara leant in and lowered her voice, "I love you so much. I wish I could spend every minute of my waking day and night with you. Sometimes I can't even find the words to describe how I feel about you, because when I try, I come over all emotional."

"Aw, that means a lot to me. And I feel the same about you, Cara. I can't think of anyone else at this precise moment I want to be sharing my fish and chips with." Scott grinned cheekily.

Cara pinched his thigh. "You're such a romantic."

They continued to tuck into the rest of their fish and chip supper, savouring every last mouthful, with Scott wishing he'd chosen a larger portion of chips instead of the regular size.

Cara rested her elbows on the table. "I wonder if the girls were living a double life their parents didn't know about?"

Scott tilted his head. "How do you mean?"

"Well, the picture they painted at home and at school may not have reflected reality. From what you're saying, LSD isn't an easy drug to get hold of. You said yourself Mike struggled to find any dealers who could get their hands on it. That suggests to me perhaps only one or two people, or perhaps a small handful, have access to LSD."

Mike had struggled to track down supplies of the drug and continued his search as an ongoing priority.

"Where are you going with this?" Scott asked, his curiosity piqued.

"Perhaps you're looking in the wrong place. What if they didn't acquire the drugs from someone in school? Few people have access to it, so what's the likelihood of a fifteen- or sixteen-year-old lad getting his hands on LSD?"

"Well, it's just as likely that someone much older than a schoolkid supplied them with LSD."

Cara nodded and shrugged a shoulder. "It's a possibility.

A very plausible one. Maybe you need to look at their wider friendship circle, anyone in their late teens and early twenties. That would certainly be a good starting point, don't you think? There are lots of girls of that age who tend to act older. They don't want to be seen as a fourteen- or fifteen-year-old schoolgirl. You look at the way they dress up when they head into town on a Saturday afternoon." Cara grabbed her phone from her handbag and pulled up Google. She punched in a few websites and showed them to Scott. "It's hard to tell a fourteen year old from a nineteen year old sometimes, especially when they've done their hair and makeup and dressed in clothes they bought from websites like these. Misguided and Boohoo are really popular with that age group."

Scott acknowledged Cara's point of view. As he pondered it and the evidence, there was a strong case for his team to focus on who the girls may have come into contact with outside of school. He had seen the posts that the girls had placed on their own Instagram pages, and on reflection, Cara was right. They certainly looked much older when they dressed in casual clothes. And the before and after shots of them doing their makeup certainly made them look much older. If he hadn't known them, he would have guessed the girls in their photographs were in their late teens.

Scott had a new spring in his step as they left the chip shop. Cara's insights had opened up a new line of enquiry in his mind, one that would require him going back over old ground.

22

Grief. It was a powerful emotion.

He hadn't experienced it personally, but it had felt like that at times whilst growing up. And as he drove down the street, past Kitty's house and then on to Claudia's, he wondered about the depth of their parents' grief.

Children – no doubt school friends – gathered in the gardens, lighting small candles and huddling together for comfort and warmth, their faces illuminated by the orange glow of naked flames that danced in the evening breeze. They struggled to keep their crying silent, looking up to the watery, dark skies and the heaven beyond. Their shoulders shook. Tissues wiped away their snot.

He cruised by slowly, keeping an eye on his speed. He didn't want to attract attention, but he equally wanted to see the fuss he had created. He imagined both sets of parents felt empty. Filled with nothingness that had robbed them of life. If that was the case, then he had done the right thing.

It was their fault. They'd spawned evil bitches who'd

preyed on the weaknesses and vulnerabilities of others. The parents should have taught them right from wrong, but they'd failed in their job. The world had no room for kids like them. As he turned out of Claudia's road, he imagined her parents sitting on the sofa, crushed by a wave of agony. They probably felt like the weight of the world was resting on their shoulders and there was nothing they could do to lighten it.

He had kept his feelings and memories buried for years.

It was all their fault, those silly little bitches. If it hadn't been for them he would have lived his life, made the best of things, while his memories remained locked away in a box deep within his mind. But it was their fucking fault. Years of therapy and counselling had unravelled because of them! Their behaviour had triggered this reaction in him – a powerful force that brought a pounding to his brain.

Salty tears flowed, unchecked from his eyes.

The official mourning hadn't yet begun and already he was tired of it.

23

The last few days had left Scott drained, but he'd woken that morning with a sense of urgency and energy that had him rushing into work, ready to break the back of the case. His evening with Cara had been a pleasant distraction from work, even though they'd thrown theories and counter-theories about on their way home. Cara would always offer a different and neutral perspective, which often gave him a fresh impetus. But something else had him feeling different this morning.

His life was out of balance. He was a sucker for punishment and would spend all his free time in the office if he had his way. But Cara had a way of changing his perspective, and nudging him, often without realising, into spending more time away from the office and taking better care of himself. If he hadn't been with Cara last night, he would have gone home to an empty house and made himself a few slices of toast and a cup of tea for dinner before staying up until the early hours watching TV and channel-hopping.

This morning was different. He arrived at work, made

himself a bowl of porridge topped off with blueberries, and took a coffee on the go. He stood in front of the whiteboard, spooning mouthfuls of delicious, thick, creamy porridge whilst freewheeling his thoughts on the random scribbles and notes accumulated over the last few days.

Smiling faces of Kitty and Claudia stared back at him. The team had printed off a few more light-hearted images from their Instagram pages and added them to the board. There were pictures of Kitty with several friends having a sleepover, all of them dressed in onesies and crammed into one bed for their group selfie. Pictures of Claudia reflected similar moments of joy. One in particular showed her standing in Churchill Square a few weeks ago with friends all doing V salutes and sticking out their tongues.

A report from Matt was sitting in Scott's inbox when he'd arrived in. Feedback from Kitty's necklace found partial prints and one complete print. There were no matches on the database. Interestingly, analysis identified traces of calcium sulphate dihydrate, a common ingredient found in fertilisers and many forms of plaster.

"Morning, guv."

Scott glanced over his shoulder to see Mike skirting through the desks, eating a bacon and sausage roll, which smelt great. He was untidy and unshaven. Mike looked like he'd been dragged backwards through a hedge.

"What the hell happened...?"

"Don't mess with me. I know karate, judo, ju-jitsu, kung fu, and twenty other dangerous words," Mike snarled and cleared his throat.

"You look a mess."

Mike looked down at his attire and ran a hand through

his stubble. "Yeah, sorry about that. A late night. I was out and about making enquiries about LSD."

"Oh, yeah? How did you get on?"

"It's starting to become more popular. It was a popular in the eighties during the house and rave scene and then died down. It's made a resurgence in the last year or so as a recreational drug on the club scene. I couldn't find any dealers who supply it, but I'm going to keep looking."

Scott continued with admin for the next hour, responding to emails, and updating case file reviews, whilst the rest of the team arrived and busied themselves. He checked his phone and locked his computer screen before grabbing his jacket and dashing off to the mortuary. Cara should have finished the post-mortem and he was keen to get the results.

Scott took a few moments to examine Claudia whilst Cara finished dictating her notes. The young girl's body was twisted and mangled. Skin had been torn off her body due to her being dragged along. She had suffered multiple fractures. Cara confirmed the extent of her injuries would have resulted in instant death. She'd counted over forty breaks, massive internal bleeding from a ruptured spleen, and less than fifteen per cent of her brain matter remained.

Whilst Scott sifted through Claudia's belongings, Cara confirmed they had taken nail scrapings and tissue and blood samples. Everything she owned was torn, tattered or bloodstained. A scarf, blazer, tights, and school skirt all carried the evidence of the impact.

Scott checked her blazer pockets and found two bus ID

cards in her breast pocket and sweet wrappers in one of the larger pockets, along with a paper printout of her school timetable. He pursed his lips and studied the bus IDs. One was in Claudia's name, the other in Mia's. Scott stopped his examination when an item of jewellery recovered from Claudia's body drew his gaze. It was a necklace with a heart-shaped pendant. If he wasn't mistaken, it looked identical to the one he'd discovered in Kitty's bedroom.

Scott excused himself as he needed to head to Causeway secondary school. He went outside and called Abby about the necklace and bus passes. He asked Abby to contact Claudia's parents to confirm whether the necklace was a gift from them, and if not, if they knew how long she'd had it.

A NERVOUS ENERGY filled the corridors as Scott made his way to the main hall. The news of pupils being interviewed had spread around the school like wildfire, and a combination of panic, intrigue, and anxiety currently rippled through the student population. Raj had drafted in uniformed officers to help, and desks had been set up in the hall, spaced out to give students a degree of privacy as they answered questions. Raj and Helen conducted a few interviews but spent most of their time collating the various statements and sifting through them.

Scott made his way to the corner of the hall where Raj and Helen, camped on uncomfortable plastic chairs, were sifting through several statements. The table was already scattered with empty teacups and water bottles.

"How are you getting on?" Scott asked, as he grabbed a spare chair. He pulled it alongside Helen.

Helen drew in a long breath and exhaled. "Slow progress at the moment. No one saw anything suspicious, and the feedback we've had so far has been mixed about both girls."

"Such as?"

"Both were popular girls but tended to hang around in a small group," Helen replied.

"Don't tell me, Kitty, Claudia, and Mia?" Scott suggested.

Helen nodded before continuing. "It appears individually they were okay and behaved themselves. It's when the three of them got together that they became a handful. In a group they were louder, aggressive, and full of themselves."

"I got the impression they tended to pick on others when they were together," Raj added.

"Where's Mia now?" Scott asked.

"She's being kept at home by her parents, guv," Raj said. "Mia's too upset about Kitty and Claudia. To be honest, a lot of the kids are pretty cut up and shocked. Not surprisingly really. Her parents are in touch with the counselling team assigned to the school, and Mia's already spoken to one of the counsellors."

"Okay, keep me updated. I think it's time I had a chat with Mia," Scott said. He headed off to find the headmistress.

The school buzzer went off as he walked towards Mrs Glanville's office. Pupils spewed out of each classroom, heading in different directions to their next class. A youthful energy swirled about them, with the chatter of dozens of conversations, the animated faces, the smiles, laughs, and faces of despondency. The entire spectrum of human emotion was being played out in the corridors.

With so much innocence surrounding him, Scott reflected on how life would change for many of them when they left the safety and security of their school and moved onto the next phase in their life.

Scott waited a few minutes in Mrs Glanville's office, staring out of the window at the school playing field and the row of trees lining the boundary. From this perspective, the school grounds appeared to extend far behind the main building, which gave him another thought. Somewhere beyond the treeline lay the A27. Making a mental note that he needed to follow up on, he was interrupted by Mrs Glanville's return.

"Here are Mia's details," the head said, handing Scott a slip of paper with Mia's address and the names of her parents.

"Thanks. What are her parents like?"

"If you're asking whether you'll be welcomed or have the door slammed in your face, I'd go with the former. I've met them a few times on parents' evenings. Both *appear* nice enough. Her dad is French. Mum seems to be the chatty one of the pair, but I'll let you make up your own mind when you meet them."

24

Scott checked the address a few times before stepping up to the door and ringing the bell.

The door opened a few inches. A chubby face peered out, dark eyes framed in large, round tortoiseshell glasses. The woman blinked a few times as she chewed on her bottom lip.

"Yes?"

"Mrs Boswell?" Scott asked.

She had a worried look. "That's me. I'm Angela. You are?"

"Detective Inspector Scott Baker of Brighton CID. May I come in? It's in connection with the recent tragic deaths at Causeway."

Angela nodded and showed Scott through to the lounge. "Can I get you a drink? Tea, coffee or water, perhaps?"

"A black coffee, no sugar would be great, if it's not too much trouble?"

"Sure, no problem. I won't be a minute, so please take a seat," Angela replied, before scooting off to the kitchen at the rear of the property.

Scott heard the kettle being flicked on and the familiar hissing and bubbling sound. A TV played in the background, muted for Scott's benefit. An old episode of *Countdown* had reached the conundrum round. He was in a homely room, with family photos that fought for every square inch of space on the mantelpiece above the fake fire. Comfy sofas that might swallow you up were arranged in an L-shaped configuration to one side, and a beech laminate floor and white walls offered a contemporary feel to the space.

Angela walked in slowly, keen to avoid spilling the steaming hot liquid.

"Here you go," she said, handing the mug to him.

"Thanks, that's perfect."

She held out a small white plate with a decent selection of Bourbons, digestives, and jammy dodgers, which Scott politely declined.

"Sorry for the intrusion, Mrs Boswell–"

"Call me Angela," the woman interrupted.

"Right, Angela. Also sorry for the short notice, but as I said over the phone, I want to ask Mia a few questions. I'm investigating the deaths of both of her friends, so anything she can tell me about their interactions might help our investigations."

"I'm not sure she's in the right place to help. She's hardly uttered a word since it happened and rarely comes out of her bedroom. The counsellor who turned up earlier had a right nightmare trying to get through to her. The poor woman had to go away but promised to come back a little later." Angela glanced up at the wall clock.

"I'd like her to stay at home with you for the time being," Scott said. " It's the safest place for her, and I imagine she doesn't want the extra attention at school right now."

"Safest?" Angela asked, her brow creasing with concern.

Scott didn't want to alarm the woman further so softened his stance. "By that I mean she's lost two friends, and right now, she needs to be comforted by her parents. With you keeping an eye on her, any changes in her mood or behaviour can be assessed quicker. Most kids love their bedrooms and if she feels happier being cooped up in there, let's leave it at that for the moment?"

She nodded. "Oh, right. That makes sense. Well let me go and get her for you."

Scott listened to the heated argument that followed. Though it was muffled through the walls, he could make out Mia's protestations about not wanting to see anyone.

"Here is Mia for you, Inspector," Angela announced a few minutes later as she ushered her daughter through the doorway and towards the sofa.

Mia lowered herself into the seat and looked at Scott through doleful eyes. He noticed the look of terror in them.

"Hi, Mia. I'm one of the police officers looking into what happened to your friends, Kitty and Claudia. There's nothing to be worried about. We are asking everyone in your year group questions about the two girls. But I thought I'd speak to you personally because you were good friends with both of them. Is that correct?"

Mia bit her bottom lip and nodded. "Am I in trouble?"

"No, no, nothing like that," Scott reassured her.

"Then why are you here?" she snapped.

Scott noted how quickly she had turned from being terrified and looking lost to biting his head off. Though she spoke quickly, he noticed she had a slight lisp. She narrowed her eyes in defiance at Scott before folding her arms across her chest and sitting back in the cushions, like a petulant teenager. Her dark, shoulder-length hair hung across her front, partially covering her face.

"As I said earlier, it's because you were good friends with them. I thought it would give us the opportunity to talk privately without anyone hearing. We want to find out more about Kitty and Claudia. Can you think of anyone outside of school they might have been hanging around with?"

Mia remained tight-lipped.

"Mia, this is really important. We need to understand what happened in the last few hours of their lives. Did they come into contact with anyone new, anyone who had come onto the scene recently?"

A wall of silence met Scott's questions. He glanced past Mia to Angela, who offered him nothing more than an apologetic shrug. Scott had hoped a word from her mum might help, but she too remained silent.

He exhaled in frustration, expelling all air before composing himself and trying a different tactic.

"Do you smoke, Mia, or have you ever used drugs?" Scott asked. He noticed the tiny flicker of one of her eyelids as she looked at him. She lowered her gaze to the floor.

Now he was getting somewhere.

"Did Kitty or Claudia smoke or experiment with drugs?" The fact Mia didn't look up and tucked her hands under her lap told him everything he needed to know.

Scott continued firing questions at her, pleading with her at times. He explained how two sets of parents had been left devastated by the loss of their daughters. They deserved answers, and more importantly closure, which would allow them to mourn. Angela finally chipped in, but despite her best efforts, Mia refused to answer any further questions, claiming she knew nothing else.

Scott knew not to push it, and decided he'd tackle her again tomorrow with the help of an officer better trained to start a dialogue with minors.

His anger and frustration simmered as he marched back to his car. He had never found it so hard extracting information from a minor before, and at times, it felt like the investigation was going round in circles.

A quick update call in the car with Raj and Helen revealed that many of the students had mentioned outside Stop Out and the chippie was the place to be. Several of the older students had mentioned it was a place to get off your face, but none of them would elaborate further.

Armed with that new information, Scott called Abby and told him to meet him there, as a new thought percolated in his mind.

25

It was late afternoon by the time Scott met up with Abby. The quiet parade of shops they had visited before had taken on a whole new lease of life. Schoolkids were milling around in small huddles, laughing and teasing each other, with the odd chip being thrown from one group to another.

Scott walked to the edge of the pavement and checked the road. He confirmed his suspicions when he saw the empty silver gas canisters and used balloons scattered along the edge of the road. He re-joined Abby who was standing some distance from the parade. Together, they observed the children, and more importantly, looked out for any signs of drug dealing.

Satisfied there wasn't any, they headed for Stop Out, which was considerably busier than when he had last visited. School boys crowded around the different arcade machines, their faces buried in the screens, yanking joysticks from left to right. They howled with laughter.

Billy was behind the counter serving pupils when Scott

approached.

He looked up and offered them a smile as he served his last customer. "Hello, Inspector. Back again so soon?"

"Just following up on our previous visit. We plan on visiting all the shops along here. Is it always this busy?" Scott asked.

"Pretty much. It can get even busier than this, to the point where you can't even move in here. Especially when the weather is shit outside."

"Is your boss here? He hasn't been in contact with us," Scott asked, as his eyes darted around the shop.

"Yeah, he's upstairs. Let me buzz him." Billy reached under the counter and pressed the bell.

Several minutes later, Duncan Prowse came through a back door and eased himself behind the counter next to Billy.

"Boss, this is the police officer who visited last time. He said he wanted to catch up with you as well."

Scott and Abby introduced themselves, presenting their warrant cards, which Duncan examined closely. He offered the smallest of smiles and introduced himself. Scott put him in his mid to late thirties. He was slightly overweight with thinning hair, but dressed fashionably. He wore tight jeans and an open-neck shirt, which had been pristinely ironed.

Scott asked both men questions about anything they might have seen within the shop or outside. But it soon became clear Billy had a better grasp of the day-to-day running of the shop, and their surroundings.

"Mr Prowse, are you aware of kids talking about or exchanging drugs either inside or outside, because there are an awful lot of gas canisters on the road?" Scott asked.

Prowse shrugged. "I've not seen anything personally, but

then I'm not down here often. I'm generally upstairs doing the paperwork. Billy's your man in that sense. He's got his finger on the pulse and knows the kids a lot better than me. If I knew of anything like that taking place in my shop, I'd kick them out straight away. That kind of thing can get your business shut down, can't it?" he said sharply.

Scott asked again if they had seen anyone acting suspiciously. His question was met with muted responses. Nevertheless, Scott pushed on and asked whether they had seen Kitty or Claudia talking to anyone who wasn't a schoolkid, or seen any disturbances. Again, both men shook their heads, claiming they didn't pay much attention to anything outside.

It wasn't long before Scott and Abby moved next door to the chip shop in search of Kristos, who was working frantically behind his counter to serve the growing swell of schoolkids queuing up for food. His food was flying out the door quicker than he could get it out of the fryer, which meant he had little time to answer questions. In between serving customers, he managed to give his attention to Scott, who asked the same questions he had asked next door. Kristos commented that he attracted a lot of passing trade, so there were always new faces turning up in the shop, many of whom weren't schoolkids.

Scott asked if there'd been any trouble, to which Kristos replied there had been occasionally. He recalled a fight about a week ago.

"That's the problem," Kristos commented. "You have kids from two or three different schools congregating here. Many know each other, and they are always busy looking at their phones. All that Snapchat and Instagram stuff. I don't understand all of that," he said, waving his arm in the air. "But occasionally we get a bit of trouble."

Scott asked him to elaborate further as Kristos returned to his counter to pull more fish out of the fryer and empty a fresh bucket of chips in. A bubbling sizzle erupted when they hit the hot oil.

"All I remember is seeing a big commotion outside and then a big crowd bunching up because something was kicking off in the middle of it."

"And you didn't go out to break it up?" Abby asked, making a few notes.

Kristos shrugged. "I didn't have to. Before I could do anything about it, Dale rushed outside and dispersed them. All the kids broke off in different directions."

Scott looked around at the half-completed building which meant part of his shop had been sealed off with plastic sheeting. "Is Dale here today?"

Kristos shook his head. "No, the two men were waiting for supplies, so they're working on another job today."

Scott thanked him for his time before moving on to the hairdresser and convenience store. The Asian owners of the convenience store moaned about frequent shoplifting by the schoolkids. Even though a sign on their door stated no more than three schoolchildren in at a time, they were often overwhelmed with numbers and found controlling them hard. The owners pointed out their English wasn't fluent, and they found it hard dealing with the children, who would mock their accents. Scott felt a degree of sympathy for them. He had heard similar comments from many small shopkeepers, especially the newsagents and small convenience stores. Scott noticed an absence of CCTV outside, and cameras covering the inside as they left.

They drew a blank at the hairdresser, much to Scott's frustration. A woman in her fifties ran it with one other stylist. They generally kept to themselves, and their trade was mainly customers over the age of fifty-five, something she classed as the blue-rinse brigade. Scott understood why; the shop appeared dated inside.

The pungent aroma of perm lotion and hair shampoos caused Abby to scratch her nose. It was the same smell in every ladies' hairdressers up and down the country. As they left, Scott commented on how the smell was choking him and irritating his nose, to which Abby replied it was either the smell of chemicals or a dozen farts from old ladies with flatulence problems. Scott burst out laughing at Abby's observations.

So far, the enquiries had revealed mixed results. Scott had hoped for something a bit more concrete, but they were still missing vital evidence and he felt his hope fading as they ventured into the last shop. It was the electrical supplies store at the end of the parade. The owner introduced himself as Dave Whelan, proprietor for over twenty years.

"I'm Detective Inspector Scott Baker, and this is my colleague, Detective Sergeant Abby Trent. We are making enquiries in the local area following the deaths of two schoolgirls from Causeway secondary school."

Whelan grimaced. "Yes, I heard about that. Bloody tragic. So sad. I know one of the dads, Alan Morris. He pops in here every so often for supplies. A really nice bloke."

Scott agreed with Whelan's sentiments. "Have you noticed any trouble outside, or anyone acting suspiciously, especially when the schoolkids gather?"

Whelan's eyes widened. He threw a hand over his mouth. "Crikey, you think it started out there somewhere?" he said, pointing outside.

"Well, at the moment, we are simply making enquiries.

We know both of the victims spent a lot of time after school and at weekends hanging around outside with friends, so we wondered if you'd seen anything out of the ordinary."

Whelan shook his head. "I don't think I've seen any problems. It's very noisy out there when there's a big group of them. And there's a bit of argy-bargy every so often, but I've never seen any police in attendance, so I can't imagine anything serious has happened."

Scott nodded at the window. "I noticed CCTV outside when I came through the door."

"I have to. I keep a lot of stock here, and we've suffered a few break-ins in the past. Each time they hit us they disabled the alarm system and cleared us out. I've recently upgraded my security measures and installed CCTV footage, for both front and rear."

That was the first bit of good news Scott had heard all afternoon. "I don't suppose you've got footage for the past seven days, have you?"

"As a matter of fact, I have. It's on a thirty-day loop. After thirty days, the tape gets wiped and starts re-recording again."

"Do you mind if we get a copy?"

"Sure, no problem. Give me a minute," Whelan replied. He disappeared into the back room.

The more Scott thought about it the more convinced he was Mia was holding something back. She knew more than she was letting on. With CCTV footage in their hands for the last thirty days, he could see for himself what the kids were up to, and more importantly, if Kitty or Claudia had been in contact with anyone who may have supplied them with drugs.

26

They faced a mammoth task. Abby and Scott pulled up two chairs around a video monitor and began reviewing the CCTV footage from the electrical store. With over two hundred hours of footage capturing a view from the front and back of the store, they finally had the opportunity to see the final moments of when Kitty and Claudia were last seen alive.

Mike wheeled another chair beside them and dropped his heavy frame into the seat. He caught his breath.

Scott glanced at him. These days, Mike was often out of breath just moving from one end of the CID floor to the other. Mike had packed on more weight in recent weeks, putting it down to the Christmas festivities. Scott was concerned about Mike's general health the more he listened to his laboured breathing. He made a mental note to have a quiet word when the opportunity arose.

They spent the next few hours watching the comings and goings outside the parade of shops. The occasional delivery or postal van would turn up to drop a few parcels at the electrical store or convenience store. There appeared to be a slow, but continuous stream of women going into the hairdresser. The builders at the chip shop would often come out for a quick cigarette break in the alleyway behind the shops.

Scott made sure he and his officers took frequent breaks. It was vital they remained focused. From experience, he knew staring at a video screen for too long would result in fatigue and tired eyes. Mistakes happened then and vital information could be missed. So they took turns, making sure two people were always present and watching the screen.

Abby returned with a bottle of water and a small pastry. "There's such innocence in kids. They have it quite easy, but they don't realise it until they turn into adults and get burdened with relationships, kids, money worries, paying the mortgage, cooking, cleaning, and generally getting fucking old."

Scott agreed as he watched a small gathering of kids swell. The schoolkids moved amongst different groups – boys teasing the girls, and the odd chip being thrown between the small splinter groups. It was harmless fun, and as darkness descended, the groups continued to mill around, everyone reluctant to go home.

The footage captured Kitty, Claudia, and Mia several times. On each occasion, Scott slowed the footage and zoomed in, so they could get a better view of each girl, and more importantly, who they were talking to. Whilst Scott studied the interaction between the girls, Mike kept an eye on passing traffic, and anyone hanging around in the street observing the children from a distance. Mike had already checked for any locals on the sex offenders register with an unhealthy interest in girls of school age. With two such individuals on their patch, Mike had printed off their photos and kept them beside him as he scanned the screen.

"There," Abby said, jabbing a finger at the screen. The three of them watched the next few minutes play out, before replaying it. It showed Dale stepping out to talk with Kitty and Claudia. As they continued to play the footage covering the next few days, the same thing happened. Dale was seen talking to both girls, sometimes as part of a group, sometimes individually.

"I thought Dale said he had nothing to do with the kids?" Abby said.

"He did. He implied he had nothing in common with them," Scott replied. "Jailbait is a term I think he used. He did say Kitty had been a bit flirty. Mike, get him in for a chat. Let's see why he's not being entirely truthful with us."

"It looks friendly enough, and they seem comfortable around Dale," Abby continued.

Both girls visited Stop Out on several occasions, and after checking the timestamps, Scott realised they'd been in there for over an hour on each visit. From what they observed, the average length of visit for most kids going into Stop Out was between forty-five and ninety minutes.

The team counted at least a dozen occasions where Dale had spoken to at least one of the girls. As the frequency of conversations increased, some took place in the alleyway behind the shops where both girls were seen laughing and talking with Dale. Nothing in their behaviour suggested they were distressed, concerned, or worried about their safety.

The evening began to drag as they continued trawling through the footage. Further insights of significance showed Dale and Billy sharing a cigarette break behind the shops on many occasions. The body language between them implied they got on well, but other than that, nothing else of importance was flagged up.

"Listen, guys, we've done enough of this," Scott said, stretching his neck from left to right. "I don't know about you but I'm shattered. Let's call it a day. The night shift can continue reviewing the footage. If there's anything of importance, they can give me a call."

"That sounds like a great idea. With a bit of luck, I can grab last orders and get a quick pint or two on my way home," Mike said, pushing back his chair and dashing from the room.

"Mike's life seems to focus on drinking and eating," Abby commented. "Do you think he's stressed, or is it something he likes to do?"

"Have you noticed any changes in his behaviour?" Scott asked.

Abby shook her head, but added drinking had been a large part of Mike's life when he was in the army and it was still his way of relaxing.

Scott followed Abby out of the building and towards the car park. As the cloudless sky sent temperatures plummeting, he stopped beside her car and pulled up the collar on his coat, to shield himself from the worst of the winter chill.

"Are you up to much tonight?" he asked her.

"I'd love to say I'm gonna have a hot warm bath, throw on a thick pair of pyjamas, and curl up in bed and fall asleep. The reality is I'll go home, tidy a pile of dishes the kids have left in the sink, run around the house clearing up after them, and make sure they have done their homework."

Scott smirked. "The joys of being a working mum."

"Something like that. I'll see you tomorrow."

27

In the darkness of a nightmare, his mind would conjure up the worst magical beasts, with razor teeth like a piranha. They would move in unnatural ways; maybe they would limp or be severely hunched over, or drag their feet. Soon the calm breathing would become gasps. On awakening, despite the nightmare ending, a ghastly feeling of being watched by something invisible would prolong his uneasy feeling.

He gasped as his body jolted him from the nightmare. His clothes clung to him, drenched in sweat. He had fallen asleep to the sound of music playing in the background, Before long, the recurring nightmare had surfaced once again, dragging him to a place he would much rather forget. It was the same most nights, since those bad memories had been unlocked.

For so long he'd kept those memories buried, along with the nightmares. His experiences as a child had left him scarred and angry. He still hated the way they all laughed at him, taking the piss out of his weaknesses and his inability to stand up for himself. The nightmares had started not long after and had continued for a few years until he'd left school. Once away from his antagonisers, he had moved on. The memories had faded, and the nightmares had petered out.

He stared at the ceiling, knowing he needed to continue his work. For the first time in his life, he had the power. He enjoyed exploiting their vulnerabilities and giving them a taste of their own medicine. For all intents and purposes, they may as well have been attacking him, but seeing them pick on others was the trigger he needed to follow his current path.

Throwing his legs off the side of the bed and sitting up, he knew his job was nearly done. He got up and stood in front of the mirror, running his fingers over the remaining scars. A constant reminder of his past. As he'd grown older and bigger the scars had shrunk in size, barely visible from a distance.

A reminder chimed on his phone while he stared at his reflection. It was time to set off and find his next friend.

He threw on a jumper and tapped the back pocket of his jeans, to make sure he had what he needed.

As he walked towards his front door, he picked up the open jewellery box sat on the shelf. He stared at the pendant and chain inside and smiled.

She will love it.

28

E xcitement bristled amongst the team as they arrived for their shift. Overnight, officers had continued trawling through CCTV footage from the electrical store, as well as the surrounding area. It was the first credible breakthrough for the team since beginning the investigation. News had also come through that, following Scott's request, the night shift had located Dale, and he'd be arriving shortly.

Scott and the team crowded around a large television Mike had wheeled in. Abby perched on a desk close by, whilst Mike, Raj, and Helen settled into chairs in a small arc in front of the TV screen, notepads at the ready. Scott positioned himself behind them. He folded his arms across his chest and rolled his bottom lip through his teeth as he watched the movie. Deep down, he prayed the night shift was right and had indeed found a connection with the drugs.

The HD footage itself was clear and began with a view above the alleyway running along the back of the shops.

Several cars were parked in a long line. Officers confirmed they belonged to Duncan, Billy, and Kristos. On occasion, a battered white Transit van was seen parked behind the chip shop, which officers confirmed belonged to the builders. A second van was parked behind the electrical supply store, and with its liveried sides, had been identified as belonging to Dave Whelan, the owner. Confirming who the vehicles belonged to was great, but Scott's impatience grew as the minutes ticked by.

Following a period of inactivity, a silver Ford Focus came into view and took the unusual step of reversing into the alleyway for its entire length before idling for a few minutes. The team held their breath, waiting to see what happened next, but when the car drove out of the alleyway, they let out a collective groan.

"That's a bit of an anti-climax," Raj muttered under his breath. He let out an exasperated sigh.

Mike nodded. "It was, but the vehicle belongs to Craig Fletcher, a dealer from Hastings with connections in the Brighton and Hove area. He is known to police. He has a girl-friend and a little kid over in Kemptown."

"Mike, send officers to pick him up. Try his girlfriend first, and if he's not there, speak to officers in Hastings and get them to rattle his door. He could be the one who is dealing LSD and that's why you drew a blank with local dealers," Scott said.

Mike leant over the desks and called the duty sergeant.

The team continued to analyse the footage as new evidence surfaced of Dale talking to lots of schoolgirls on several occasions, with particular sightings of him talking to Kitty, Claudia, and Mia. Scott noticed how he was often surrounded by up to half a dozen girls whenever he stood outside the front of the shops, but his behaviour changed when he saw either Kitty, Claudia, or Mia around the back. He became more animated, standing closer to each of them, occasionally placing a hand on their arm or around their shoulder. Jakub occasionally popped his head out of the door to check on his workmate before darting back in. He appeared to have no interaction with the girls, and with his poor command of English, he likely kept himself to himself.

Scott and Helen pulled themselves away from the TV when Mike's desk phone rang. The call uniformed colleagues had picked up Dale Walsh and he was being held in an interview room. As Scott made his way downstairs the footage bothered him. The more they analysed it, the more questions it threw up. Clips had surfaced of schoolkids chatting with Billy by the back door of Stop Out, and Duncan occasionally joining them.

Was it something innocent? Or was there more to it? Scott needed to know fast.

"Am I under arrest?" Dale chuckled nervously, as he took a sip from the tea provided for him.

Scott and Helen took up their positions across the table from him, and after introducing themselves for the benefit of the tape, Scott rested his elbows on the table and let Dale's question hang in the air for a few seconds.

"No, Dale. You're not under arrest. You're helping us with our enquiries. You are entitled to legal representation should you wish, and you can leave this interview whenever you choose to."

On hearing this, Dale let out a noticeable puff of air, and relaxed back in his chair, his cockiness returning.

"I'll keep this short and sweet," Scott began. "When we first spoke to you, you said you had nothing to do with the girls who hung around outside the chip shop and Stop Out. The word used was jailbait."

Dale shrugged. "Yeah? And?"

"We have obtained CCTV footage of you talking to several girls, both on the main road and behind the parade of shops where you're working. Any reason why you chose to lie to us?"

Dale cleared his throat and shifted uncomfortably, pretending the seat was too hard. "Dunno. It must have slipped my mind."

Scott exchanged a small glance with Helen, who was making notes. "It slipped your mind that you had spoken to several girls, two of whom are now dead?"

"Hold on a minute, hold on. That's got nothing to do with me. I'm probably one of dozens of people they spoke to in the last few weeks."

"Yes, you're probably right, Dale. But from the footage we've viewed, you may have been one of the last to talk to either of those girls." Scott threw out the suggestion as he wrote down the dates of when Kitty and Claudia went missing. He turned the note around to face Dale. "Where were you on these dates?"

Dale's eyes flickered before narrowing. He stared at the piece of paper. "I don't know. Not off the top of my head."

"Not good enough, Dale. Think harder," Scott pressed.

Dale ran a hand through his hair, his usual cockiness deserting him as he pursed his lips and thought hard. "I swear I had nothing to do with them. I work. Yeah, chat a bit.

I dunno." Dale rambled and tripped over his words. He looked at the dates again. "I was at the gym after work on the afternoon you say Kitty disappeared. As for Claudia, I was at home. I didn't have to be in work until a bit later, so I had a lie-in."

"We will need to check to confirm these details," Scott replied.

"Yeah, but I live with my mum and dad. I don't want them freaking out. They've seen these girls on TV. I don't want them getting upset with you telling them I had something to do with their disappearances."

Scott reassured him they would be careful and sensitive, as he made a note of Dale's address, and the name of the gym he attended.

"Dale, do you take any drugs?"

The change in direction startled Dale. He picked up his tea. The cup trembled in his hand. His nerves were clearly getting the better of him. "A bit."

"What do you take and how often?" Scott asked.

"Only a bit of weed. But mainly at the weekends. I like to smoke a bit before I head out for the night. I never do any in the house; my old man would go fucking mad."

"Where do you get it from?"

Dale shrugged. "Wherever. Whoever is selling it."

"Names?" Scott asked, his tone clipped.

Dale claimed he didn't know names, just faces. Just people he bumped into in pubs and bars but no one he considered friends.

"What did you talk about when you spoke to Kitty and Claudia?"

"Nothing in particular. Just banter. Stuff like how school was, and what they were up to at the weekend."

"Did you ever offer them drugs?" Helen chipped in.

Dale shook his head furiously. "No way. I'm not getting into trouble for supplying them. I get a bit, but that's for personal use," he said, holding his hands out defensively.

"Were you involved with any of them sexually?" Scott continued.

"What... Are you kidding me?" Dale protested, his voice rising with each word. "They were kids. Can you imagine what would happen if I got caught having sex with a school-girl? Are you mad?"

Scott ignored his protestations. He pulled still photographs from a Manila folder and placed them on the table for Dale to see. "Here are images of you getting quite close to both girls. As you can see, you place your hand on their arm or around their shoulder on more than one occasion. Is that all you did?"

Dale threw his hands up in the air. "Fucking hell, you're reading way too much into this. I'm telling you, it was harmless chit-chat."

Due to the circular nature of Dale's defensive ramblings, Scott terminated the interview not long after. He was satisfied he'd rattled Dale's cage enough for the time being. Helen would organise a set of prints and a DNA swab to be taken for elimination purposes.

Scott's day went from bad to worse when he left the interview room to find Raj outside.

"Sir, Craig Fletcher did a runner before officers arrived to pick him up."

29

Information was coming in from all sides as Scott returned to the CID floor. Abby waved him over and provided him with an update on the calls she'd made. Following a recent conversation with Mrs Glanville, the headmistress reported there had been instances in the past where children were found in possession of drinks and drugs, but she'd been quick to point out that such events were infrequent and were dealt with effectively.

"Do you know what kind of drugs?" Scott asked.

"From what I can gather, very small amounts of weed. Year Ten boys were discovered at the back of the field smoking the stuff." Abby checked her notepad before continuing. "There was no police involvement, and the matter was dealt with between the school and the parents. Those involved were suspended."

"Anything else?"

"A couple of issues in the past involving the possession of penknives. How did you get on with the interview?" Abby asked.

"We've got a Jack the Lad who thinks he's a bit special. I got the impression he enjoyed the attention from the schoolgirls. We need to check his alibi for the evening that Kitty disappeared, and for the morning Claudia didn't arrive at school."

"There's definitely more going on than we are aware of. Mike went through more of the footage. Do you remember when Kristos told us about a disturbance outside?" Abby asked.

Scott nodded. "The one where Dale went out and broke it up?"

"Yep. Well, it turns out that it was more than a little scuffle or disagreement. The key instigators were Kitty and Claudia."

Scott raised a brow in surprise.

Abby looked shocked too as she continued. "They were pushing around another girl. And soon, a whole crowd was gathered around them. They were really having a go at her. There is audio on the recordings but the cameras are too far away to pick up a normal conversation. You can clearly hear the screaming and shouting. The word 'shank' kept coming up."

It had been a while since Scott had heard that phrase; it took him back to his days in Essex. Shank was a common word used amongst gangs on the estates. It meant to stab someone.

Scott instructed Mike to speak to Kitty and Claudia's parents, to find out if they knew about their daughters being involved in fights. In the meantime, he needed to go back and have another chat with Billy.

IT WAS quiet when Scott arrived at the parade of shops. The shutters were up on Stop Out, and Billy was restocking the confectionery shelves in readiness for trade later on. Scott tapped on the glass door, startling Billy, who spun on his heels to see who it was.

"Inspector, your visits are becoming a habit," he said as he let Scott in. He picked up the empty confectionery boxes and took them through to the back.

Scott followed him. "I'm following up on a few more enquiries. We've been looking at CCTV footage from down the road which captures both the front and rear of this property, and I wanted to ask a few more questions."

Billy nodded as he unlocked the back door and took out the rubbish. Scott followed him outside and looked up and down the alleyway. It was relatively clean, with large, industrial wheelie bins behind each property. A large stack of empty oil drums sat behind the chip shop, and the smell of fried food lingered in the air.

"What do you want to know?" Billy asked, slapping his hands together to clean them.

"We noticed that you spent quite a bit of time talking to schoolgirls, predominately out here," Scott began. "Any reason for that?"

"Not in particular. We get a bunch of schoolkids meeting up outside and sometimes round the back here."

"You seem to get on well with them. Some of them are a good bit younger than you. Do you have a keen interest in one or two of them?" Scott asked, studying Billy's reaction closely.

Billy pulled a packet of cigarettes out from his back pocket and lit the tip of one. He took a deep drag and blew out smoke rings. "I get on well with them. That's about it. I think they like the fact that I've got a car. When they stand here, I open up the car and put on my sounds. I think it makes them feel a bit older hanging out here than around the front with the rest of the kids."

"Did you see Kitty or Claudia hanging around with anyone else that wasn't from their school?"

"I only ever saw them chatting up Dale."

"Chatting up?" Scott asked.

Billy smiled and shrugged. "Yeah, I think they were keen on him. Definitely a bit of flirting going on there."

"What makes you say that?"

"They were acting all cute and silly around him. You could see it in their eyes. They fancied him."

Scott tilted his head to one side. "And Dale reciprocated?"

"I guess so. He was definitely giving some back."

"Do you take drugs, Billy?"

"Nah, that's not for me. I'm already doing a great job of knackering my lungs with this shit," Billy said, staring at the glowing tip of his cigarette.

"Did you know about the fight that took place a few days before Kitty went missing?"

"Yeah. Duncan went out to break it up. It's happened a few times. You get a couple of the boys flexing their muscles and getting a bit lippy. And the girls tend to be quite bitchy. They're often fighting over the boys," he said, shaking his head.

Scott made a mental note of Billy's response as he continued to ask a few questions, including his whereabouts at the time both girls disappeared. His answers seemed plausible. Scott made a note of them, confirming he would check it out.

Billy continued to take deep puffs on his cigarette, keen to finish it. He flicked the butt into a bucket of water. After, he walked over to his black BMW one series and wiped building dust off the bonnet, likely from the work being done on the chip shop. He tutted, clearly annoyed.

"If there's nothing else, Inspector, then I need to get back to work. The floors all need washing."

"No, that's it for the moment. I'll get back to you if there's anything else I need," Scott replied.

He glanced into the bucket to see dozens of fag butts floating in the blackened water. That didn't bother him as much as the glimpse he caught of discarded roaches or cannabis butts, scattered a few feet away.

30

He'd been careful, ensuring he stayed away from the scenes as much as possible, but his macabre curiosity made him drive past their houses under the cover of darkness to see the commotion and devastation left behind by the tragic "accidents". Each time it filled him with satisfaction knowing his actions had created so much attention. In his twisted mind, he enjoyed it.

Took pride in it.

Relished it.

Rejection hurt. Why should others get to smile, laugh and have fun when that was all he'd ever wanted... but never had the chance.

Available. Vulnerable. Desirable.

Those words had described him back then and had made him an easy mark. He'd made himself available, drifting from one group to another, in a desperate attempt to be accepted, to be wanted. But those actions had left him vulnerable, highlighting his weaknesses, and because of that, he'd become a highly desirable target in the eyes of his attackers.

A soft target.

These girls – the so-called victims – had willingly sought out someone similar. They'd thrived on the weakness of others.

There were plenty of cameras and CCTV across the town, and to make sure he wouldn't be caught, he had walked many of the routes himself, deciding which streets were safe to drive down, where he could park, and when would be the best time to meet the girls. Whilst they were looking for him, he was somewhere they hadn't even considered.

He stared through his windscreen as life continued around him. Pensioners shuffled up and down the road, heading for the nearest shops to pick up the small essentials they needed. He watched an old lady lean over a large, boxed shopping trolley. Its squeaky wheels alerted everyone to her presence. Each step she took looked painful.

She's probably got arthritis, or an ungodly disease is eating away at her body as she nears the end of her life. He hoped he would not end up like that – old, frail and lonely.

His car was parked in a long line of cars along one side of the street, inconspicuous to everyone who passed by. A large overhanging tree, its branches, though devoid of leaves, cast gloomy shadows over his car, shielding him and his passenger.

"I'm scared. My mum's going to go mad when she finds out." Mia's voice was barely audible.

He turned and offered her his most reassuring and sympathetic smile. A smile he had given her many times.

"Listen, it's absolutely fine. There's nothing for you to worry about. You're safe."

"But... but, I'm sad Kitty and Claudia have died. They were my friends. I don't understand what happened. What if there's a complete nutcase out there? Others are talking about how they were both killed by an axe murderer with scars on his face."

He smiled to himself. He tried his hardest to stifle a laugh. It amazed him how vivid kids' imaginations were, how easy it was for them to twist reality until they became terrified of their own shadows.

"Seriously, do you think I would be out here if there was an axe murderer killing people? That's kids trying to scare each other. Besides, with them out of the way, you now have your chance. Kitty and Claudia, well, they were silly girls. But you're much more grownup than them, and that's why you didn't hang around with them as much. They were always fighting for attention and wanting to feel special, but he told me he liked you more than any of the others."

Mia paused and considered his words. She turned to face him. "Really?"

His eyes widened in encouragement. "Yeah. But he couldn't let the others know. He thought they weren't quite right in the head, and so he didn't want to upset them by telling them. They were so silly and naïve. Surely you must have realised that yourself? I noticed you didn't stand near them as often, and you acted differently. That's because you're more grownup. You still fancy him, don't you?"

Mia hesitated, pulling her coat tighter and wrapping her arms around her chest.

"Mia?"

She finally nodded and pursed her lips.

"He'll be so excited to hear that. Don't worry about the others. They weren't right in the head, which is why they did what they did. When they realised that he didn't fancy them, they tried to get his attention, but it went horribly wrong."

Mia stared out the window, deep in thought. "Does he really fancy me?"

He nodded excitedly. "Yes, he said it to me again yesterday. He fancies you the most. And it's you he wants to keep safe. I reckon he loves you."

Mia blinked her eyes furiously. "Why didn't he meet me today, then? Why you?"

"He wanted to meet you but was out picking up supplies for the shop. He asked me to fetch you, so you would be waiting for him when he got back. He said he couldn't wait to see you."

Confusion clouded her eyes. She clearly wanted it to be true; so much had happened in recent days. "I really need to get to school, I'm going to be in so much trouble," she said, unzipping her coat to check her phone.

He reached into the side pocket of his door and pulled out a little jewellery box. He handed it to her. "He asked me to give this to you."

Her small, delicate hands opened the box. Inside was a silver necklace with a heart-shaped pendant. She stared at it for a few moments, stroking the pendant.

"It means you're special," he said, "but you must hide it. No one can see it yet."

She smiled knowingly, before shutting the box and placing it in her rucksack.

"Oh, by the way, he gave me this to pass to you," he said, handing her fifty pounds. "Said you could go out and buy a new top on Saturday before coming over to the shop. How does that sound?"

Mia nodded enthusiastically. She had likely never held fifty pounds before. She stared at the money as if it were precious gold.

"Listen before you head back home, I picked up a bar of chocolate and a drink for you, in case you were hungry or thirsty. Let me get them from the boot." He hastily opened his car door and the boot and retrieved a bag. He opened the can of Red Bull and slipped a tablet in, swirling the can around so as to dissolve it quickly, before returning to his seat.

He handed the can and two chocolate bars to her. "Here you go. He wasn't sure exactly what you liked, so there's a couple of things there. Put those in your bag, and get this down your neck."

"I'm not really thirsty," Mia replied.

"I know, but it's open now, so you might as well have it. You can throw away whatever you don't drink. Go on... you'll love it."

Mia tentatively took the can. She'd tried Red Bull once before and had enjoyed the taste. She sniffed the contents before sipping it.

He was right. She did love it, and though her mum warned that energy drinks were bad for her, she had seen a lot of the older boys pouring vodka into their cans outside Stop Out on a Saturday night.

He smiled to himself.

Not long now.

31

After receiving the dreaded call, Scott raced back to the office. He tore through the building to CID. Support officers were furiously typing on their keyboards; others sat with their phones cradled on their shoulders whilst making enquiries.

"What have we got, Abby?" Scott asked, his breaths heavy.

Abby relayed the most pertinent points. "Mia Boswell has disappeared."

"What do you mean disappeared? She was at home for fuck's sake! Her mum said she rarely left her bedroom!"

"I know. According to her mum, Mia was in bed, so Angela grabbed a shower. When she checked on Mia fifteen minutes later, her bed was empty and the front door was unlocked. Mia isn't answering her phone, and her mum is going out of her mind. It isn't hard to figure out why."

"Any signs of a forced entry?" Scott asked as the muscles in his neck tightened. His head began to ache.

Abby shook her head.

This was the worst news Scott could have received. Uncovering the reasons for the suspicious deaths of Kitty and Claudia was challenging enough, but Mia disappearing raised the stakes even higher. Meadows had already paid Abby a visit whilst Scott was out, furious at the lack of progress, and panicking over the shit storm about to hit them, once the media found out.

Scott walked over to the map of Brighton at one end of the room. "Have we got any ideas as to where she might be?"

"Not at the moment, guv. I've classified this as a high-risk MisPer, and I've flooded the area with extra officers. They are combing the surrounding streets and neighbourhood."

"Where's Raj and Helen?" Scott asked as he looked around the floor.

"I've dispatched them to Mia's parents first, and then they are going to join the search."

Scott agreed with the action steps implemented already, grateful for Abby's swift decisiveness. He stared at the whiteboard and circled Mia's picture. They needed to find her fast. They didn't need another body. But finding her in a population of over six hundred thousand people with such limited resources, and even less time, was going to push them to the limit.

"Where are we with the rest of the investigation?" Scott asked, as he turned towards Mike and Abby, who were standing behind him.

"We've downloaded Claudia's phone log," Mike began. "There were a number of calls made to Kitty's phone, but no evidence of text messages. I imagine she was using What-sApp or something like that. There were a few calls to her mum and dad."

"Was that it? Nothing else?"

"No, guv. Claudia had received seven calls over the last two weeks from an unregistered number. I can't trace it. But here's the interesting thing, I cross-referenced it with Kitty's phone log and she had five calls from the same number. The numbers don't match any belonging to those already logged from interested parties in this investigation."

"Mike, I know we are pushed for time, but let's see if we can access Mia's phone logs as soon as possible, and cross-reference that unregistered number."

"Yes, guv. I'll sort that out now."

"Anything else?" Scott asked, as he picked up the nearest phone, ready to make a call.

Mike added. "I spoke to the parents. I asked whether they knew if their daughters were involved in any fights recently. Both parents were unaware of any such incidents."

Scott thanked Mike and called the owner of the chip shop. In his conversations with the man, he had logged conflicting information. Scott needed to confirm whether Kristos's assertion that Dale had gone outside to break up the fight was accurate, because Billy had contradicted him.

He spoke to the man. Kristos sounded deeply apologetic and confirmed he must have been confused, because it was indeed Duncan who'd gone out to break up the fight.

Scott was still listening to Kristos's apologies when Abby took another call. Abby's eyes widened and she slammed down the phone. Scott cut the conversation short and promised to call Kristos back later, just as Abby charged across the CID floor to him.

She relayed the message that uniformed officers had attended a call from concerned security staff on Palace Pier moments ago. The security officers had stopped a young girl from jumping off the end of the pier. Initial reports suggested the teenager was in a state of disorientation and unfazed by her antics. With concerns for her safety, she had been taken to the hospital after collapsing and slipping into unconsciousness. A library card retrieved from her purse confirmed it was Mia Boswell.

THE PAEDIATRIC WARD at the Royal Sussex County Hospital wasn't a place Scott or Abby visited often. Mia had been placed in a small room to the side of the ward, while a uniformed officer stood outside the door. The smells of disinfectant and the aroma of cooked food lingered in the air. Scott and Abby were shown to the far end of the corridor by a nurse. Colourful paintings and pictures of children playing, along with palm trees and animal murals, softened the hospital feel of the ward. Lions with smiley faces and zebras with big, cheesy grins stared back at them as they passed by beds.

It wasn't a place Scott wanted any child to be, but many patients appeared upbeat, as the nurses and care assistants hovered around each bed, making a fuss of the children.

Scott and Abby presented their warrant cards to the officer on duty, who acknowledged both of them.

"What can you tell us, officer?"

"Guv, Mia Boswell is unconscious at the moment. It sounds like she took something; they've taken bloods and are fast-tracking the analysis. The attending officers confirmed she was seen entering the pier smiling and was later observed with her arms extended out, as if she were flying."

"And still smiling at the end?"

The officer looked surprised at Scott's question.

"It's a simple question, officer. When the security staff stopped Mia and held her till officers arrived, was she still smiling?"

"Oh right, sorry, guv. Yes. The pier security team, concerned by her behaviour, followed at a discreet distance. They caught her clambering over the railings behind the fairground attractions."

Scott closed his eyes for a moment as he imagined Mia falling into the sea and being dragged under the steel pillars. There had been several occasions where holidaymakers had leapt off the pier only to be dragged below by the swirling undercurrent.

The officer retrieved a large, clear evidence bag, which he passed to Scott.

Inside was Mia's rucksack. It weighed considerably more than expected.

Scott snapped on a pair of latex gloves before opening the plastic bag and unzipping the rucksack. Three red bricks were inside.

"Shit. She would have gone down in seconds," Scott whispered. He looked up at Abby who shook her head.

Scott and Abby walked into the room. Angela Boswell shot them a glance through bloodshot eyes, pain etched on her face. She cradled her daughter's hand as she sat beside her.

"Angela, I wish we were meeting again under different circumstances. This is my colleague, Detective Sergeant Abby Trent. We appreciate it's a difficult time for you but can we ask you a few questions?"

Angela Boswell pursed her lips and shook her head

before resting it on the bed. "Why? Why, baby, did you do this?"

Soft cries filled the room. She was overcome with pain and emotion. Scott watched as the woman's life shattered into a thousand pieces in front of her eyes.

After giving a respectful pause, Scott asked, "Angela, was there anything in Mia's behaviour which concerned you before she disappeared? Did you hear her talking to anyone on the phone, something of that nature?"

Angela shook her head, not taking her eyes off Mia. "I wish I could help you, Detective Inspector. I promise, Mia rarely left her bedroom." The woman's voice broke. Tears flowed down her face. "This is all my fault, isn't it?"

Scott wished he could take Angela's pain and regret away, knowing all too well how it felt to blame oneself for failing to protect your child. "No, it's not. Rest assured we're working day and night to find the person responsible."

Abby nodded for Scott to join her outside.

"Guv, let me hang around here. Perhaps she'll open up to me in the next couple of hours. I can't imagine we'll get much out of her at the moment. I'll get a couple of teas organised."

Scott knew Abby was right. The shock was too raw for Angela Boswell to cope with.

The officer informed Scott that Mia's father was on his way, which might give Angela the added support that she needed. Abby promised to keep Scott updated whilst he headed back to the office.

32

The image of Mia lying unconscious lingered in Scott's mind as he sat in his office chair and tilted his head back. The need find the person who'd targeted these three girls had become even more pressing. The question he kept returning to was why?

Had they been targeted for a specific reason, or was this the tip of the iceberg and more victims would follow? There was a serious risk that this could escalate, leading to more teenage victims in the morgue. It wasn't a thought he cared to entertain; the repercussions would be beyond unimaginable.

Everyone in the team doubled their efforts to track down the supplier. Meadows organised several uniformed officers to be assigned to CID to keep a lid on this, as pressure from the media increased. The press team were being bombarded for statements and explanations as to what they were doing, all the while insinuating this case was too big for them to deal with.

Dale's alibis had checked out, much to Scott's disappointment. CCTV overlooking the front desk at the gym showed Dale checking in at three forty-five p.m., and leaving at five twenty-five p.m. His parents had confirmed he was at home on the evening of Kitty's disappearance and hadn't left the house. He had also been at home and sleeping in on the morning Claudia went missing.

Scott continued to scribble down these points on his notepad. He'd hoped his notes would give him a few insights, but he was sadly mistaken. He blew out his cheeks and stared at the mass of squiggly lines and names that littered his page.

Scott was interrupted when Helen tapped on the door.

"Guv, have you got a minute?"

Scott threw his pen down on the table in frustration and waved her in.

"I can come back later if it's a bad time?" Helen suggested.

Scott shook his head. "No, don't be daft. Sorry, I'm not pissed off by your intrusion. I hate it when there are so many loose ends." He drummed his fingers on the table, as if this mere act would conjure up an instant solution for him.

"Well, maybe this will help. The guys have been trawling through so much CCTV footage that I think they'll have square eyes. Anyway, they found a very short clip which shows Billy giving Kitty a long hug at the back of the shops. And then he does the same with Claudia about twenty minutes later. And in both clips, he is seen kissing both on the cheek."

"Shit," Scott said, wide-eyed. "Was it a lingering kiss or a quick peck? Though both could be seen as inappropriate."

"A bit in between. It's neither. But here's the interesting thing. They found another short clip where Billy is with

Kitty and they move nearer to the hairdresser that, unfortunately, is away from the cameras and out of shot for about ten minutes. Billy reappears in the footage, looking over his shoulder and smiling at someone who we believe is Kitty. He is seen puckering his lips and blowing her a kiss. They cross-referenced it with surveillance footage from the front of the shops, and Kitty is seen about the same time reappearing on the main road, so it looks like she walked around the back of the shops and re-joined the rest of the kids."

"Cheeky fucker." Scott fumed. "There's a lot more going on there than he's told us about. He's been playing the girls."

"And he's been playing us as well, guv."

SCOTT PACED AROUND the CID floor, getting updates from the various officers and their individual lines of enquiry. Other officers had been dispatched to track down Billy and bring him in. One way or another, Scott wanted answers, so when officers confirmed Billy was waiting in an interview room, Scott wasted no time in heading down there, taking Helen with him.

Billy looked more frustrated and annoyed at being called in than anything else. Helen did the formal introductions and cautions before Scott commenced the interview.

"Is it going to take long?" he snapped. "Because I'm not sure why you brought me in. You've been over to the shop a few times already, so surely I've given you everything you needed?"

"You've been very cooperative, Billy, but perhaps not so forthcoming with the true facts," Scott replied.

Billy shrugged and said he couldn't think of anything else that would be of interest to them.

"Billy, did you ever make contact with Kitty, Claudia, or Mia by phone? Did you send any text or WhatsApp messages?"

"No, why?"

"Mind if we check your phone logs?" Scott asked, nodding at Billy's phone that was on the desk alongside his bunch of keys.

"No. You can't check my phone. It's private. You said this is voluntary and I can leave whenever I want to. I'm not under arrest. So what's your game?" Billy fired back, his bravado returning.

"Further evidence has come to light that you were friendlier towards Kitty and Claudia than you claimed." Scott slid still images across the table of him hugging and kissing Kitty and Claudia.

Billy shrugged again. "It's just a bit of flirting. They know what they're doing. It's not like I got into their knickers or anything like that. As I said, I can easily go out and trap on a Friday night, and they'd be a lot older than those kids." He jabbed his finger at the still images.

"I don't buy that, Billy. You see, I get the impression you quite liked the attention, perhaps even encouraged their infatuation towards you. And you've been exploiting it for your own gains."

"Hold on a minute. What the fuck are you suggesting?" Billy snapped. He hammered his fist on the table.

Scott wanted to push his buttons more. "I think the girls wanted to act a lot more grownup than they really were, simply to get your attention. Call it a schoolgirl crush. And you lived up to that crush. You let them hang out with the big boys around the back of the shop. You let them sit in your car, listen to music, you gave them a bit of *extra* attention and perhaps supplied them with drugs?"

"Jesus fuck, maybe I do need a solicitor if you are going to throw around accusations like that."

Scott lifted a shoulder. "Your phone is there. You're free to call anyone you want to. I'm only interested in finding out who supplied the girls with drugs. Did you supply them?"

"No!" Billy shouted.

"I noticed a lot of roaches littering the floor round the back of Stop Out when I last spoke to you. Did you supply Kitty or Claudia with marijuana joints?"

Billy shook his head and stared up at the ceiling. "No," he replied defiantly.

"The impression I'm forming here is this little parade of shops is more than just a meeting place for kids to hang out after school, and share a portion of chips or a can of Coke. It's more than a place where kids can play retro arcade games and have a bit of a laugh. To me, it looks like a place where the vulnerabilities of children are exploited. It's a hotbed of adolescent hormones and impressionable kids, and I'm wondering if you had a part to play in all of this?" Scott leant back in his chair and folded his arms across his chest, whilst he observed Billy's behaviour.

"Find the evidence to prove it. You've got it all wrong, and until you can find anything else, this interview isn't going any further." Billy grabbed his keys and phone and stood up.

As Scott watched him go, Billy's words rang true. Scott needed the evidence to hold him, and what he had was nothing more than circumstantial.

NEEDING A BREATHER FROM THE OFFICE, Scott left Helen to oversee things in his absence. He threw on his coat and headed out for a quick walk, to get some fresh air. As he left the station building, he punched in Abby's number.

"How are things at the hospital?" Scott asked.

"Unfortunately, there's no update on Mia's condition. Doctors are checking on her and she's on a drip at the moment. Her dad arrived not long ago. It was heartbreaking, guv. They were sobbing their eyes out and had me going for a minute as well. I stepped out of the room to give them a bit of privacy."

"I bet. Did you get a chance to talk to Angela at all?"

"I did a bit. Mia doesn't have a boyfriend, at least no one the mother is aware of. She has a small circle of friends and latched on to Kitty and Claudia when they showed a bit of interest in her. I got the impression she kind of went along with it because those two girls were popular."

Scott wondered if Mia was easily influenced. "Did she mention anything about changes in Mia's behaviour?"

"Not recently, guv. She did say Mia came out of her shell a bit when she began hanging around with Kitty and Claudia, but then things turned sour."

"How so?"

"Mia told her mum Kitty and Claudia weren't very nice people and had started to pull away from them, but felt pressurised to stick with them. Mia thought the girls were bullies and sometimes took things a bit too far. Though Mia didn't say this directly to her mum, Angela got the impression Mia often got goaded into taking part whenever they picked on others."

"So, we have a couple of popular girls who liked to pick on others, and thought themselves a bit special?"

"It sounds a bit like that, guv. Or perhaps it's just girls being girls and bitching about each other. It does happen. I've lost count of the amount of times Sophie's told me about how bitchy some girls are at school."

"Okay, Abby. We really need to speak to Mia. She holds the key, but there's not much we can do at the moment. Why don't you knock off and leave her parents to spend some time with her? I'll see you in the morning."

Abby thought that was a good idea. She agreed to say goodbye to Mia's parents before leaving.

33

Scott returned to his office to find Matt leaning over his desk. He was jotting something down on a Post-it.

"Ah, Scott, I was leaving you a note. The tox report came back on samples taken from Claudia. Unfortunately, traces of LSD were found in her bloodstream, though you've probably already guessed that."

"Pretty much. It was a likely conclusion but we needed it confirmed anyway. At least there is a clear link to drugs in both cases now. The kids are being supplied with drugs, and the likely source is going to be someone near to the parade of shops based on feedback from pupils at the school, the sighting of Fletcher around the back of the shops, and Dale being a social user of cannabis."

"Well, I'll leave it to you. Happy hunting," Matt replied. He waved as he left for the evening.

Scott picked up his phone and dialled Duncan Prowse's number.

Surely, he must know something about the drugs being peddled in the local area?

Scott sighed when there was no answer. He made a mental note to try again later as he headed to the main floor.

"Guv, Mike was looking for you earlier," Helen shouted from across the desks.

"Any idea where he is?" Scott said, looking around the empty desks.

"Try the canteen," Helen replied. "He said he was hungry not long ago, so the chances are you'll probably find him down there."

Scott made his way down to the canteen and scanned the room for Mike. Uniformed officers sat in small groups, taking the opportunity to have a quick bite to eat during their shifts. Others sat alone, spread out in various corners, reading a book. He noticed Mike at the cashier's and waited by the doors for him to leave.

"I was going to come find you, but I thought I'd grab myself something to eat first," Mike said with a smile, waving a white polystyrene sandwich box. "Lasagne and chips, sorted."

Scott laughed. "Trust you to think of your stomach first, Mike."

"An army marches on its stomach. That was always drummed into me in the army."

Scott and Mike walked back to CID.

Scott paused by Mike's desk, as Mike planted himself firmly into his chair. He flipped open the lid to his food, and began tucking in. He updated Scott at the same time.

"Guv, I had a uniformed officer catch up with me a few moments ago, and as part of the ongoing enquiries on the door-to-door stuff, an elderly resident showed them some useful information. This old fella has CCTV which looks out across his front garden and to the road beyond. The good news and by sheer luck, his camera also captures the alleyway behind the shops."

Mike shovelled an enormous portion of lasagne forked with chips into his mouth. Feeding time at the zoo was a thought that sprung to Scott's mind.

"Are you going to finish the rest of the story, Mike?" Scott pushed him.

"Oh, yeah. The old fella referred to footage that was captured about ten days ago of suspicious activity taking place behind the shops. He's a bit of a nosy fella and likes to keep an eye on things. He wrote down the registration number of the car that was stopped behind the shops. It turns out the registration he gave me belongs to our dealer, Fletcher." Mike took another large mouthful before continuing. "I've seen the footage. It shows Billy walking up to the driver's door. They speak for less than thirty seconds, and it looks like there's an exchange. Billy pockets something and walks back into Stop Out and Fletcher drives off."

"I don't like this. I don't like this one bit." Scott fumed. "Someone is lying, and I'm sick and tired of it. Get a warrant organised. I want you to go and arrest him on suspicion of supplying and then search the shop and his bedroom."

"What, right now?" Mike asked, looking at his food.

"Yes, Mike. Now. I can't believe we've just spoken to him. I'm heading back to the shops to see if I can get in. With a bit of luck Billy or Duncan will be there, so I can start a search. Get uniform to meet me there!" Scott shouted, as he headed off to get his coat.

THE ROADS WERE empty by the time Scott reached the parade of shops. The chip shop was still open, with a few people milling around outside. At this time of the evening, all the teenagers had gone home.

Scott peered through the shutters of Stop Out. It was dark inside and there appeared to be no sign of movement. He was joined by two uniformed officers who pulled up outside and waited for his instructions.

Scott dialled Duncan's number again, only to get his voicemail. He decided to call the station, with a request to send a unit to his home address to pick him up. Scott instructed one of the officers on the scene to remain at the front of the building whilst he and another officer headed to the alleyway behind the shops. They both flicked on their torches in the darkened space. Beams of light bounced off the walls and wet ground. Scott's light picked up Billy's vehicle near the far end of the alleyway.

The warrants Mike had organised meant Scott could seize Billy's car and look for any signs of drug activity.

Scott's radio crackled into life. "We've got a runner. He's heading in your direction," said the officer at the front of the property.

Scott spun on his heels and raced down the alleyway, towards a road that would take him around to the front of the shops. As he approached the end of the alleyway, a darkened figure came into view. He stopped upon seeing Scott, before turning and running away.

"Police! Stop right there!" Scott shouted. All three officers joined the pursuit on foot.

The hooded figure charged across the road and vaulted over a front garden wall then ran along the front of a row of houses, taking each small, dividing fence with ease. Scott and the officers chased after him. Scott moved quicker than his uniformed colleagues, who were weighed down with heavy utility belts and radios.

His feet slipped on the wet winter leaves as he ran along the pavement; the cold evening air shocked his throat and lungs as he inhaled deeper, faster. He soon narrowed the gap between himself and the runner, as bins were tossed in his way to slow him down, and small wooden fences were pushed to one side as the figure charged through them.

Alarmed residents appeared at their front doors; curtains twitched.

Scott was within touching distance of the runner when he launched himself at him. The pair crashed to the ground and rolled into the bushes. Scott jumped up and flipped the hooded figure onto his front, grappling with the man's hands to pull them behind his back. The heavy thud of footsteps came up behind them. The man's breath came out in small, hot and nervous spurts.

"Stop resisting!" Scott shouted as the other officers secured the man's legs and knelt on his back.

"Get the fuck off me!" His words were muffled.

"Calm down. You're making this much harder than it needs to be. Stop resisting," Scott repeated.

"You're fucking hurting my wrists!" The man screamed.

"If you stop moving, it won't bloody hurt."

Scott finally managed to secure the man with handcuffs. He yanked back the man's hood. He rolled his eyes. "Billy, you're starting to get on my nerves. We only just spoke to you."

"I haven't done anything wrong. This is harassment!" Billy screamed, protesting at the pain and injustice.

"Stop being a big baby!" shouted one officer, as the sound of approaching sirens interrupted.

Scott arrested Billy on suspicion of supplying a class B drug before placing him in the back of a police van. Within moments, the street had become a hive of police activity as officers dealt with concerned questions from residents. A tow truck took away Billy's car, and a search was conducted of both the road outside Stop Out and the alleyway, in case Billy had dropped any evidence.

During the search, a large amount of building materials was discovered under a tarpaulin sheet. Scott watched as a few officers sifted through the material under torchlight. They uncovered discarded rubble, half used bags of plaster, and several stacks of red bricks.

The red bricks drew Scott's attention as he stepped in for a closer look. They bore the same LBC imprint to signify the London Brick Company and carried the same unique, indented texture on the bricks found in Mia's rucksack.

34

Scott placed one foot in front of the other, careful not to spill his surprise, as he padded towards his bedroom. He shifted his eyes from the breakfast tray to the door.

Don't spill it, careful, don't spill it.

The idea had seemed great to begin with; the execution left a lot to be desired. His heart hammered in his chest and his mouth dried, as the anxiety mounted. He watched the tall, thin glass of orange juice rattle on the tray, threatening to turn an act of love into a catastrophe.

He pushed open the door with his knee and tiptoed around to Cara's side of the bed. He set the tray down on her bedside table. She stirred at the sound of rattling crockery. Her eyes flickered awake and she placed a hand over her mouth to stifle a yawn. She looked from Scott to the tray then back to Scott again, her brow furrowing in confusion.

"Anniversary?" she asked.

Scott shook his head and smiled.

"Um... Birthday?"

"Nope."

"Because I'm an amazing girlfriend and great in bed?"

Scott rocked with laughter and placed a soft kiss on her forehead.

"So... what's this for?" Cara asked, her eyes travelling back to the tray beside her.

"I guess it's my way of saying sorry I've not been around much, and for not giving you the time you deserve."

Cara smiled affectionately, staring into Scott's eyes. "You have nothing to be sorry about. You and I both know the pressures of the job. I don't expect to see you much when you've got a big case like this. I thought you knew me well enough to know I'm not one of those nagging girlfriends who demands attention."

"I do, but it doesn't make me feel any better. This case is doing my head in, and because of the age of the victims, it's messing with me a bit." Scott stared at the wall for a few seconds.

Cara rubbed the back of his hand. "You're only human. And besides, you know I'm always here for you. We both have very tough jobs, and we may not get as much time together as most couples, but we understand that, don't we?"

Scott nodded appreciatively.

"Anyway, it's about time I was treated to breakfast in bed."

"I'm always treating you to breakfast in bed, Cara."

Cara shook her head. "I didn't mean *that* kind of breakfast, but now you mention it..."

"It's not going to happen today, beautiful. There's been a development up at the school, so I need to head there first. But in the meantime," Scott said, retrieving the breakfast tray and placing it on Cara's lap, "you have fresh orange juice, coffee, toast with your favourite jam, and a boiled egg."

Cara's eyes widened. She licked her lips. "I guess this will have to do if I can't have you." She took a sip of her orange juice and savoured the refreshing taste.

"Indeed," Scott said. He headed for a shower, before dressing and scooting out the door, leaving Cara to finish her breakfast at leisure.

PUPILS WERE ALREADY at their lessons by the time Scott arrived. He'd deliberately waited until school had started before turning up to meet Mike at the gates. They were joined by Mrs Glanville, who was bundled up in a thick coat, with a chunky scarf wrapped around her neck.

"Good to see you again," Scott said, greeting her with a handshake. "Has Mike filled you in?"

"He has. I haven't seen it myself. Mike suggested the three of us look at it together, if that's okay?"

"Of course. Mike, can you lead the way?"

"Follow me, guv."

They followed the outdoor path through the network of school buildings until they reached the school playing fields beyond. To the left was a football pitch. The grass had been turned over, and a muddy quagmire remained where studs from football boots had left their mark. To the right was another pitch, less used, but showing signs of recent activity. Scott imagined pupils would congregate here in small huddles during their breaks. The soil was so damp that worms had surfaced, and crows were flying over the grass to pick them up.

Towards the rear of the field, the grass sloped downwards towards a bramble-filled ditch, overgrown with cow parsley and nettles. It formed a natural security fence to stop unwelcome visitors, even though several feet behind it was a wire fence, which skirted the perimeter of the open land. The continuous hum from traffic on the A27 turned into a roar the closer they got.

"This way, guv," Mike instructed, taking them to a small clearing in the brambles.

Several large rocks sat in the hollow, providing stepping stones over the muddy ditch. The three of them crossed it with a bit of effort before arriving at the wire fence a few feet farther on. Mrs Glanville tutted and grimaced at her shoes, realising how inappropriately dressed she was for what appeared to be a cross-country trek.

"Look at this." Mike pointed out.

They stood beside a small opening in the fence, which appeared to have been broken for some time. Beyond the line of the fence was a grassy bank that continued for about thirty feet before stopping at the edge of a road that skirted around the back of the northern fringe of Hove.

"The search team uncovered it yesterday evening. This could be the route Kitty took when she left school. It would explain why no one saw her leaving through the front gates." Mike suggested.

Mrs Glanville looked horrified as she examined the small clearing they were standing in. She looked back at the school, her mind processing the ramifications of how a small breach in their school perimeter may have compromised the safety of her pupils.

Scott thought aloud. "It could also explain why no one

saw Claudia. This could have been the meeting place for whomever she met?"

"If you've ever had kids bunking off from school, I bet you a tenner, Mrs Glanville, this is how they get out," Mike said.

"Okay, Mike," Scott said. "Get SOCO down here. Let's see if they can lift footprints from the ground on the other side of the fence. The ground is soft and muddy, and we may get some imprints which match the footwear either Kitty or Claudia were wearing at the time of their disappearances. They may pick up a few hairs or fabric fibres that snagged in the wire."

An uncomfortable feeling settled in Scott's stomach as he left the school. Despite a few questions being answered by his visit, a new line of enquiry had opened up as well. The disappearance of both girls without anyone seeing still played heavily on Scott's mind. The discovery of the gap in the fence appeared to be the most likely exit route for Kitty and whomever she'd met beyond the perimeter of the school. A quick check of his map confirmed how easy it would have been for Claudia to take a detour that took her around the edge of the school and to the same meeting point, without being seen.

A VISIT to the hospital before returning to the station did little to cheer Scott up. Mia was still unconscious. Her parents were maintaining a bedside vigil, catching quick catnaps in the uncomfortable hospital chairs. Scott saw the pain and agony etched on their faces. Speaking through bloodshot eyes, the uncertainty of the circumstances in which Mia was found played heavily on their minds. They searched Scott's face for answers, and though he tried to reassure them, he felt unable to take away their pain.

Scott took Mia's parents into a side room and spoke to them about the prickly subject of drugs. Angela Boswell was adamant her daughter wouldn't touch drugs and was vociferous in condemning people who used them. Scott tried to reassure her there was a high probability Mia had unwittingly consumed LSD and that he was doing everything within his power to find the person who had supplied her with the drugs. The doctors on Mia's ward remained hopeful that Mia would recover and that the drugs administered to counter the LSD would soon take effect. Due to the toxicity of the substance, her heart was struggling to maintain a normal rhythm, so it was touch and go.

ONCE BACK AT THE STATION, Scott gathered the rest of the team.

"Right, I've just returned from the hospital and there is a possibility Mia might not make it. Obviously, we hope she has the strength to pull through. In the meantime, I want a full background search done on Mia. Let's find out what her movements were within the last twenty-four hours."

"Similar to the other girls, Mia was found in a very public space," Helen said. "The Palace Pier and the surrounding area has decent CCTV coverage, guv."

Scott turned to the map on the board and circled an area of about two hundred square yards, before the entrance to the pier. "We've got multiple roads converging on the roundabout before the Palace Pier. There's an elevated camera directly in front of the pier and many others scattered in the vicinity. We need to get copies of any footage captured in the last twenty-four hours. If Mia was with anyone, she may have been dropped off close by."

"I'll check CCTV, and ANPR records for any vehicles we've already logged in this investigation," Raj offered.

"Good idea. And whilst you're at it, run the same checks for where Kitty and Claudia died. Cross-reference the lot."

"Will do, guv."

"We've got Billy downstairs again, and Abby and I are going to interview him now," Scott said, grabbing his notepad and finishing the briefing. "He's had the night to think about things. I'm particularly keen to deal with the evidence we have of him possibly dealing, and his connections to a known dealer in the area."

35

The need to find Fletcher was more pressing than ever.

Scott stood outside the interview room and discussed tactics with Abby. All efforts to locate him had proven unsuccessful. Officers and criminals often played a game of cat and mouse, with those being hunted going to extreme lengths to avoid capture. He'd known of raids where officers had searched a house and not turned up their suspect, only to discover later the wanted criminal had been hiding inside an Ottoman bed, or in a deep cavity beneath the floorboards.

Despite several visits to Fletcher's girlfriend's house, officers had returned empty-handed, and the results in Hastings had been just as poor. Scott was sure Fletcher would return to Kemptown and had convinced Meadows to sign off overtime for officers to mount a surveillance operation, which had begun yesterday. With budgets being tight, Meadows could only authorise forty-eight hours, which left Scott nervously checking his phone for any updates.

The decision to leave Billy sweating overnight had been deliberate on Scott's part. He was sick and tired of being given the run around by everyone he spoke to, with the softly-softly approach doing little to further their investigation. Following Billy's arrest, a warrant had been executed to search Stop Out, with officers conducting a thorough search with a drugs dog. Scott had wanted to give the search teams enough time to uncover anything of significance, and the news they had buoyed his mood as he opened the door to the interview suite.

Billy looked frazzled, cradling a hot cup of tea and exchanging nervous glances with the duty solicitor. Scott and Abby took up their positions opposite him, with Abby doing the formalities. Scott had wanted to bring Billy down a few pegs, and an overnight stint in the cells appeared to have had the desired effect. His hair looked untidy and dishevelled, his face showed the first signs of stubble, and his eyes were bloodshot from the lack of sleep.

"How are you doing this morning, Billy? Did you sleep well?" Scott asked, smiling at Billy, his tone tinged with sarcasm.

"What do you think?" Billy spat back, not looking at the two officers.

"I trust officers in the custody suite treated you well? You'd better get used to those conditions, and hearing the metal door with its familiar clank as it's locked behind you each day. Because that's what you can expect if you don't cooperate."

"Your threats don't worry me. Trying to put the frighteners on me? Forget it. I've not done anything wrong." Venom laced Billy's tone, his words clipped and defiant.

Scott tapped his pen on the table, in no rush. He looked

at Abby as she prepared for note taking duties. She raised a brow, knowing exactly what was coming next. She felt the impending sense of satisfaction from seeing the smile soon wiped off Billy's face.

Scott locked his fingers behind his head and leant back in his chair. "You see, that's where I think you're wrong, Billy. We had officers conduct a thorough search of Stop Out during the night and guess what we found?"

Billy smiled. "Don't tell me, dozens of bars of chocolate, loads of packets of crisps, a tonne of canned drinks stored in the storeroom?"

"I'm glad you find it funny, Billy. We found a quantity of drugs under the till. A small bag with brown tablets. They looked identical to those recovered from Claudia's bedroom." Scott paused for a moment, letting the bombshell sink in. "The very same ones we believe Kitty, Claudia, and Mia were given. If proven to be the case, then the drugs seized at Stop Out will be the same ones that led to Kitty falling more than seventy feet from a bridge to her death, to Claudia stepping out in front of a bus and dying the most horrific death, and to Mia trying to jump off the end of Palace Pier. She remains unconscious in hospital."

Tension tightened Billy's expression. His eyelids twitched. He glanced at his solicitor, who whispered in his ear, advising him to respond with a no comment to any further questions.

Billy clenched his jaw.

"Have you any idea how they reacted to it?" Scott asked. "I'll tell you, shall I? It made them agitated, excited, and euphoric. Their sense of perspective on reality became distorted. They felt as if they were in such a happy place that they wanted to dance. Kitty thought she could fly. It caused them to see and hear things that weren't even there. One minute they were confused the next they were frightened, and then they were relaxed. But all the while, their tiny hearts were thundering, working overtime. They were sweating, disorientated, and yet thought they were untouchable."

Scott paused for a moment, as he watched Billy's hands tighten into fists on the table. His fingers were pushed so deep into his palms, his knuckles had turned white.

"And you supplied them with those drugs. That's why you returned to the shop after we'd spoken to you. You wanted to get those drugs before anyone found them. We've got surveillance footage of you with Craig Fletcher, a known drug dealer, and what appears to be a potential exchange of drugs behind the shops. Billy Crowther, you are in a lot of shit."

His face had a sweaty sheen to it. "You're bluffing. You're saying all this to wind me up. You can't prove anything," Billy replied.

Scott shrugged before leaning into the table. He looked Billy in the eyes. "I don't have to prove anything. That's a decision for the CPS. I just need to present the evidence. And the evidence suggests you are involved with a local drug dealer. You are also involved with girls who sadly lost their lives under the influence of drugs. If you don't start talking now, then you're going down for a very long time."

Billy twitched and squirmed in his seat as his chest heaved, clearly desperate to take in as much oxygen. Panic coursed through his body. "I swear it wasn't me. I only gave the girls weed. That's it." His solicitor placed a hand on Billy's arm, which Billy at once brushed off. "Fuck off!" He shouted at the man.

"If it wasn't you, then who was it? I need names, Billy.

And I need them now. If you're covering for someone else, then you're playing a fool's game. There're no prizes for loyalty. Trust me."

Billy raised his hands, desperate to deflect heat away from him. "Okay. Okay. I swear it wasn't me. You need to speak to Dale. He is the one who deals in charlie and weed. Look at him, not me. I don't know anything about any other drugs. I got stuff for Dale and passed it onto him."

"From Fletcher, Craig Fletcher?" Scott asked.

Billy nodded.

"For the benefit of the recording can you speak out your responses please," Abby interjected.

"Yes, from Fletcher."

Scott moved the interview on, changing direction. "And what about Duncan? What do you know about him?"

Billy shrugged. "He's okay. He's always on the phone. He opens and closes the shop sometimes and occasionally joins me behind the counter."

"Does he pay much attention to the kids?"

Billy furrowed his brow in confusion. "What do you mean?"

Scott sighed, getting tired of the interview. "I mean, does he ever watch the schoolgirls?"

"Yeah, now you mention it. I see him sometimes watching the kids outside, or when they come around the back. But he only comes outdoors or looks through the back window when the girls are there. Never when the boys turn up. I kind of think he likes to perve on the girls."

"And you didn't find that odd?" Scott asked.

"I guess. I mean, they're not even half his age, they're less than that. He doesn't do it often, not like every day. Mind you, he isn't there every day."

"But on the days he was there, you noticed him doing it often?"

"Yeah."

"Did he talk to them much? In particular, Kitty, Claudia, or Mia?" Scott probed.

Billy shook his head. "Not often."

"And where is Duncan now?"

"I dunno. He comes and goes as he pleases. He trusts me enough to open and close the shop. He says he has other business interests and people he needs to see."

"We've been looking for him, Billy. He is not answering his phone, and he doesn't appear to be at his flat. The neighbours haven't seen him for a few days. Do you have any idea where he might be?"

"No."

"Billy, if you're trying to protect him, you're going to come out of this a lot worse. This is your opportunity to make amends and be completely honest and truthful with us."

"I swear, I don't know where he is. And I don't know who the drugs belong to, either. It's Duncan's shop, so maybe they belong to him."

"Perhaps," Scott said, shrugging. "But as you've just pointed out, he's not there often, and he rarely joins you in the shop or behind the counter. So if that's the case, then I imagine you'd have more of an idea as to what's hidden beneath the till than Duncan would?"

Billy's face reddened. His eyes widened, as all exit routes began to close off. "Listen, all I know is Duncan has a couple of different places where he lives. Maybe he's at one of those. He's also got some small lock-up where he keeps extra arcade machines. That's all I know. I don't know where."

36

Scott and the team gathered to re-focus their strategy as soon as the interview with Billy ended. Drugs picked up during the search of Stop Out were being fast-tracked for analysis by Matt's team, and Scott hoped for results before the day was out. As he added a few notes to his notepad, he made a mental note to visit the forensics team.

"Let's do a quick round robin and get an update on where we are. Mike, do you want to kick off?"

"Yes, guv. I've got forensics at the school examining the opening in the fence at the back of the field. I left them to it, but early indications look interesting. They picked up a quantity of clothing fibres that had snagged on the fencing. Whether any are going to help our investigation is anyone's guess. Dozens of kids could have used that route to skip school, or access it if they turned up late after the front gates were shut."

Scott understood the predicament and now doubted they would get anything conclusive from the fibres. Their analysis alone could take days, needing to be cross-refer-enced with Kitty's clothes.

"There were plenty of footprints in the muddy ground, but again, the footprint analysis could take a while and time isn't on our side," Mike added.

"Any news on Fletcher?" Scott asked, turning to Helen. He had tasked her with being the go-between for CID and the surveillance team.

"I'm afraid not, guv. There's been no movement at his girlfriend's flat. Do you honestly think he's going to turn up there?"

"I hope so, Helen. He's been hard to find so far, and I hate slippery tossers like him. Mike, any joy with leaning on Fletcher's associates? They must know where he is."

Mike shook his head. "It's honour amongst thieves, and all that bollocks. They're never going to snitch on their own."

Scott stared at the incident board and jotted down further points as he processed his thoughts. "What car does Duncan Prowse drive?"

"A grey Honda CR-V," said someone else in the group.

"Duncan is proving a hard person to track down as well. He knows we're looking for him and the fact he's not coming forward or answering my calls bothers me." Scott turned to face his team. "Any retail owner would be concerned if there were allegations of drug dealing happening both inside and outside their shop. The fact he's staying silent seems odd."

"Maybe we need to be more proactive in tracking him down?" Abby suggested.

"That's what I'm thinking myself, to be honest. Can you run all the usual checks on him? And let's dig into his back-ground in more detail. Let's see if we can find his car and track its movements. Can you set up an ANPR alert for me,

Abby? If we can get the cell site data on his mobile number, we can triangulate his last known positions." Abby jotted down the action points whilst Scott wrapped up the team meeting and told everyone to crack on.

Scott headed down to the forensics department to have a quick chat with Matt. The department was much quieter, with people working diligently on collating samples and writing reports. It had a slower, quieter pace to the frenetic front-line policing departments where officers shouted information across desks, calls were continuously being made and received, and laughter occasionally interrupted the seriousness of the work.

He found Matt leaning over the desk of one of his assistants, in deep discussion, and pointing to information on a computer screen in front of them. Scott waited in the background for Matt to finish. Then, he pulled him to one side for a quick chat.

"Hi, Matt. I won't keep you too long, but I wondered if you had any further updates for us?"

"Yes, actually. Let's pop into my office."

Scott followed Matt down the corridor. In his office, Matt dropped into the chair behind his desk and wiggled his mouse to wake up the screen, whilst Scott grabbed the seat opposite and planted himself firmly into the chair. He glanced around the room and saw Matt had done a spring clean. The shelves were neatly lined with books. Newspapers and folders once scattered around his floor were in neat piles in one corner, and Matt's desk was sparse and minimalistic in comparison to his own.

"Now, let me have a look," Matt said as he clicked on various folders. "Ah, here it is. We did further analysis on the particles found on the necklace. Calcium sulphate dihydrate is a calcium salt used for a variety of purposes including in building materials used as drying agents, in dentistry as an impression material, cast or die, and lastly in medicine for immobilising casts."

"And of those three, which would you say is the most likely fit for the substances on the necklace?" Scott asked.

"That's hard to say. It depends on the volume of chemical components and their use. I think it's fair to say that based on what I'm reading here, they're more than likely to belong to building materials like plaster, because it's often used as a desiccant, which is a drying agent."

"That's useful, Matt. One of the suspects we've been talking to is a builder, and he's been in close contact with plaster whilst working on a shop, close to where the girls were last seen. I'll get him pulled in right away."

"It's possible there's been a transfer of dust from one site or person to another through close contact," Matt suggested.

"Are we on the right track?"

"I would imagine so, mate." Matt flicked through further reports in his inbox. "The tox reports for Mia have come back. There is evidence of LSD in her blood."

Scott let out a sigh and rubbed his temples. "Well, I guess that's good news. It indicates all three girls were drugged in the same way and would explain why their reactions and behaviour were all similar. And if Dale or Billy supplied them with the drugs, then I need to find the evidence."

37

S cott dropped Cara a quick text to let her know he was thinking of her before shoving the phone in his pocket and heading to the canteen to get a bite to eat with Abby. They picked a corner where they wouldn't be disturbed. Both of them stretched out to relax. Abby picked from a chicken salad pot, whilst Scott gorged on a BLT baguette to satiate his hunger.

"This tastes so good," Scott murmured, as he gave each mouthful an appreciative moan. "Cara's been giving me so much grief about not eating properly, and I know she's right, but we don't always have the luxury of sticking to set mealtimes."

"Tell me about it. I can go a whole day without even thinking about food."

"I don't know how you do it, Abby. You seem to survive on air. I'd pass out and slip into a coma if I didn't eat for a whole day. With the amount of training you do, and then running a busy household, whilst fitting in *this* job, I'd expect you to be eating more to keep your energy levels up."

"I do fine."

Scott knew Abby hated talking about her diet, and her lack of proper nutrition. As soon as she said the word fine, Scott knew he was treading on thin ice. That was Abby's defence mechanism to shield away any unwanted questions, and a subtle shot across his bow to warn him to back off.

Scott sipped his coffee, enjoying the taste as it trickled down his throat and warmed his stomach. If he got any more comfortable he'd probably fall asleep. He stretched out his legs and kicked off his shoes. He wiggled his toes a bit to soothe his aching feet.

"Do you reckon we'll get anything from Dale?" Abby asked, wiping a bit of mayonnaise off her lips and sipping on water. "I'm getting the impression they're all blaming each other."

"I hope so. We are running out of options now, and unless someone confesses, everything we've got so far is circumstantial. It doesn't help that Matt's team can't find Billy's prints on the bag of drugs seized from the shop."

"You're kidding?" Abby said, looking up in surprise.

"Nope. The prints don't match him, and there's no match on the system. They don't match Dale's or Jakub's either. Unless someone planted them there, the only other person I can think of who may have placed them there is –"

"Duncan," Abby said, finishing Scott's sentence.

Scott knew they needed to track down Duncan, if nothing more than to eliminate him from the investigation, but Scott sensed he was more connected to the case than they had been led to believe.

"We are running out of time, Abby. We've got officers chasing down any potential locations for him. We're running checks with the council, the banks and local private landlords, in case Duncan is renting somewhere. But it's like finding a needle in a haystack. Brighton and Hove is too big an area for us to get instant results."

"I know. It could take days, if not weeks. We could still end up drawing a blank. And there's no guarantee he's even in the area. What happens if he is away, in a different part of the country, or even abroad? His neighbours haven't seen him for a few days."

"That's why we need the cell mast data on his phone. It will give us the best indicator as to where he is, and if he's in the local area, then we will have a greater chance of pulling him in," Scott said, hopeful.

Some much anticipated news came in a short while after.

Dale Walsh had been picked up whilst travelling in the van with Jakub Novak. Much to Jakub's annoyance, his van had been confiscated by the police, to undergo a forensic search, leaving Jakub to make his own way home.

DALE'S usual cockiness was replaced by an uncertainty, which reflected his immaturity.

He glanced around and shifted nervously in his seat as Scott and Abby entered the room. A duty solicitor sat beside him, a thin poker-faced man called Terry Eager that Scott had met on a few occasions. Eager sat forward, scratching the back of his hands vigorously. Flakes of dry skin dropped to the table. The man had a bad case of eczema, and the more he scratched, the more irritated and raw his skin became. Scott hated seeing him do that on previous visits, especially when Eager would brush the flakes off the table to the floor. Scott's skin crawled.

Despite trying his hardest to eke out a confident smile, Dale's usual cockiness deserted him. He bit his bottom lip nervously.

"This is becoming a bit of a regular thing, isn't it?" Scott said, taking his seat, and waiting for Abby to complete the formalities.

"There's nothing more I can add. I told you everything I know," Dale replied, with a wobble to his voice that threatened to turn him into a blubbering mess.

"I don't think that's true, Dale. You see, we've new information to suggest you've been dealing in charlie and weed, and probably other things I'm sure you're about to tell us about." Scott raised a brow.

"Who told you that?"

"Does it matter?"

Eager placed his hand on his client's arm and shook his head, but Dale waved him away and puffed his chest out.

"Yeah, who said that shit about me?" Dale asked.

"Billy. Your friend told us you've been dealing. We want to know if you supplied drugs to Kitty, Claudia, and Mia."

"That's bollocks."

Eager rolled his eyes and stared down at his hands. He let out a long sigh, seemingly uninterested in his client's position, and said with a sniff, "My client doesn't have to answer your questions, Inspector, and has the right to remain silent."

Scott ignored Eager who he thought bore a striking resemblance to a weasel. "Billy doesn't think so, Dale. We've got him on camera purchasing drugs from Craig Fletcher, a known drug dealer in Brighton. Billy has now told us he purchased drugs and supplied them to you. It stands to reason that you perhaps supplied those drugs to the girls. Am I on the right track?"

Dale fell silent, scared that if he opened his mouth, he'd say something he'd later regret.

Scott continued. "Certain items the girls had in their possession appear to have plaster dust on them. We also have footage of you embracing the girls at different times, so it's quite possible there was transference of plaster dust to the girls. I don't believe you were obtaining drugs just for personal use, as you claimed to us during an earlier interview. I believe you were also supplying."

Dale shook his head but continued his silence.

"This isn't helping your case. Who gave those girls the LSD? Two of them are dead because of it. And you are in serious trouble," Scott continued, levelling a glare at Dale.

"Okay. Okay. I admit! I gave the girls weed and Es. I swear I didn't have anything to do with their deaths. Everyone's doing ecstasy. They were begging me to give them some. They wanted to impress Billy. They fancied him. I sold a bit of gear to a couple of the lads who were dabbling in the stuff back at school. I know it was wrong. And I fucked up!" Dale strained his voice as the words tumbled from his mouth.

"What else did you sell them?" Scott demanded.

Dale shrugged. "Not much. I swear. The occasional box of gas canisters to lads, who would then sell them on to others. But it was harmless fun."

"Let me get this clear, you sold ecstasy tablets to Kitty, Claudia, and Mia?"

"No. Just to Kitty and Claudia. They were the main ones who wanted to get at Billy."

"And what did these ecstasy tablets look like?" Scott asked.

"Like normal Es." Dale shrugged.

Scott slammed his fist down on a table, taking Eager, Abby, and Dale by surprise. The noise echoed off the walls. "I want a bloody description of the tablets! What did they have on them?"

"Inspector, such outbursts are wholly inappropriate," Eager protested.

Scott glared at the weasel.

Dale blew out his cheeks and widened his eyes, as he cast his mind back. "They had a crown emblem on them."

Scott pushed back in his chair and stood up. He paced around the room. Abby held her breath, sensing the change about to happen in his mood.

Scott slammed both of his palms on the table. He glared at Dale, his eyelids twitching in anger. "Ever heard of LSD?"

"Yeah. I do know what a tripper is. Call it what you want. Tripper, blotter, hawk, smiles," Dale fired back.

"It wasn't ecstasy you gave the girls. It was LSD. Toxicology reports have given us the confirmation. You supplied them with a hallucinogenic drug, which ultimately led to the death of two girls and has left a third fighting for her life." Scott slammed his hands down again. "You better start talking because I want answers now, and we are not leaving this room until I get them. Who gave it to you?"

"I'd seriously consider your options here, Dale," Abby interjected, "because from where I'm sitting, you're going to be spending a long time in the cells."

"An unnecessary threat!" Eager shouted. "Continue on and you'll be looking at repercussions!"

Abby ignored him with a comical snort and locked eyes with Dale.

"I don't know, okay? I got it from a geezer."

"Not good enough!" Scott screamed.

Dale held his hands out in front of him. "I swear. I didn't know it would do that to them. I didn't know it was LSD."

"I said... not... good... enough!" Scott repeated, his words slow and measured.

Dale began to sweat.

"Did Billy supply you with the drugs?"

Dale shook his head.

"Did Craig Fletcher supply you with the drugs?"

Tears threatened to fall from Dale's moistened eyes. "I swear I didn't know it was LSD."

Scott shook his head. "I need a name. I need a name now." Scott continued to apply the pressure, sensing Dale was about to crack. "A name. That's all I need. I need to know who's at the top of this chain."

Dale's shoulders shook as tears fell.

"Duncan!" he yelled and dropped his face into his hands.

38

Pleased with the result, Scott headed back to the CID room. Dale Walsh could be charged with possession and supplying to minors. Dale's desire to be popular had backfired in a big way, and Scott could only imagine the horrified reaction from Dale's parents when they were informed. Dale was eighteen and would be treated as an adult, but his parents would also be informed as a matter of formality.

The good news kept coming as Helen pulled Scott to one side after receiving information from the surveillance team. They'd seen Fletcher entering a property and were awaiting instructions. Helen had told the team to hold off until she'd spoken to Scott.

"Can we be certain it's Fletcher?" Scott shouted, racing to his office to grab his jacket.

"As certain as we can be," Helen shouted back. "The surveillance team nearly missed him because he was heavily disguised. He had the hood from his coat pulled up over his head, which shielded much of his face. He also went down a side access road between two blocks of apartments. There's a lot of people coming and going, due to most of the flats being rented out to social services."

"And then what happened?" Scott said as he returned to the floor.

"One of the surveillance officers proceeded on foot and clocked Fletcher going in the rear doors of the apartment block. Just before he went in he pulled down his hood, and that's when the surveillance officer confirmed a positive ID. His girlfriend has a ground-floor apartment."

That was all Scott needed to know. He raced from the building with Abby and Helen in tow. Though Scott wanted Abby to stay behind, part of Helen's training to take over more of Abby's work involved her shadowing Abby, so he had both join him.

Kemptown was no more than a few minutes' drive from the station. Scott pulled over into a spare parking bay overlooking the front of the apartments.

Scott grabbed his radio and keyed the mic. "DI Baker here. What's the latest?"

There was a short burst of static before one of the officers in the surveillance team replied. "Guv, no further movement since the suspect entered the property. There is no activity at the windows either."

"Roger that. Are we still certain he's inside the apartment?"

"Yes, guv."

Scott asked the surveillance team to stand by whilst they waited for uniformed backup to arrive.

"Do you think Dale was lying?" Abby asked. She sat in the front passenger seat, strumming her fingers on the door panel. Helen was in the back. Abby hated waiting around, and surveillance wasn't one of the activities she looked forward to.

Scott didn't reply, seeing the communal door on the apartment block open. His heart picked up a beat in reaction to it. He watched as an African family stepped out onto the pavement. A woman was pushing a buggy with a baby no more than a year old; she was followed by three children under twelve years of age. A thin, wiry man followed her, shouting instructions in his native dialect, and gesticulating wildly with his hands. The woman replied in an equally loud voice that Scott could hear, even though he was at least twenty yards away. The three children were oblivious to the noise, as they hopped, skipped, and jostled each other playfully. When their mother shouted at them, they froze on the spot.

"I can't see why Dale would drop Duncan in it without good reason," Scott finally replied to Abby, following the family with his eyes as they trundled off down the street.

"But why? What's Duncan got to do with this? It's Billy we saw with Fletcher. Did Billy then supply Duncan, who in turn supplied Dale? Or did Billy and Duncan both supply Dale?" Abby continued, looking for clarity in her own mind.

"That's what we need to find out. There's also the other option that Fletcher may have supplied both Billy and Duncan, but we didn't see the interaction between Fletcher and Duncan," Scott replied.

Helen sighed in the back seat, as her stab jacket stifled her movement. It pressed against her chest, restricting her breathing. "These things are so uncomfortable. I don't think I'll ever get used to wearing them."

Scott laughed. "You won't be saying that one day when it saves your life." His mind flashed back to the moment he'd discovered Sian, a former officer who had been stabbed during the pursuit of a suspect, as she lay dying in Abby's arms. It was Scott's turn to sigh as he pushed those images to the back of his mind and re-focused on the job in hand.

Backup had arrived. A squad car with three officers had positioned themselves behind Scott's car.

With the additional support of two surveillance officers, Scott had enough officers to target Fletcher. He radioed the three parked behind him, and instructed them to approach the apartment from the rear whilst the rest of the officers went in through the front door. With a communal entrance, there was a risk Fletcher would be alerted before they even got to his front door. They all exited their cars and moved off, covering the short distance to the apartment. There, they waited for Scott to make the first move.

The first few buttons Scott pressed were met with silence, but he continued to work his way through them, until one resident answered and finally released the catch on the front door. Scott and the team made their way inside to the first of four apartments on the ground floor.

Pausing for a moment, Scott checked officers were in position at the rear, and as soon as he got the confirmation, he hammered on the first door.

Footsteps could be heard on the other side. Scott positioned himself in full view of the spyhole. Abby, Helen and the two surveillance officers flattened against the walls either side, out of view. The occupant opened the door partially that was still firmly secured with the chain.

"I'm looking for Craig Fletcher?" Scott asked.

"Who wants him?" The woman replied. Her hair was untidy, her cheeks reddened, and she appeared to be wearing nothing more than a dressing gown.

Scott flashed his warrant card. "We'd like to ask Craig a few questions relating to an ongoing case at the moment."

"He's not here."

"Well, we have reason to believe he is here and hasn't left. You can either let us in or we do it the hard way."

"As I said, he's not here."

Scott's radio crackled into life. An officer said, "He's climbing out of the bathroom window. We've got a runner."

Abby and Helen were already rushing for the exit, with the surveillance officers just a few feet behind. Scott glared at the woman, who offered nothing more than a sarcastic grin. He turned and legged it back up the hallway.

Fletcher was already pinned to the ground face down, his hands being yanked behind his back and secured with cuffs, by the time Scott arrived. The scrawny man was protesting his innocence and complaining about police harassment as he was hauled to his feet by the uniformed officers.

"Craig Fletcher, we are arresting you on suspicion of supplying class A and B drugs." Scott continued to deliver the rest of his caution as Fletcher protested, thrashing between the two uniformed officers who held onto each arm.

Fletcher turned towards one of the officers and spat in his face.

The three uniformed officers jostled Fletcher to the ground before one of them placed a spit hood over Fletcher's head.

"That wasn't very nice, Fletcher," Scott said. "That's a further charge of assaulting an emergency worker, which can carry a maximum sentence of twelve months in prison. Take him back to the nick."

Before Scott and the rest of the team left, they located Fletcher's car in a small resident's car park to the rear of the block. Keys taken from Fletcher gave them to access his vehicle, which would be impounded. But to their horror, Helen located a handgun tucked beneath the driver's seat. Scott ordered armed officers to attend to make the weapon safe. The vehicle was then loaded onto a low-loader and removed for forensic analysis.

———

AN AGITATED FLETCHER sat in the interview suite, flanked by a police officer either side of him. Scott was in no mood to take chances after Fletcher had spat at the officers detaining him. He'd waived his right to legal representation and sat grim-faced, staring at the wall ahead.

Scott was joined by Helen, who conducted the formalities. Whilst she did, Scott studied Fletcher.

He was a scrawny man, with an unkempt short beard, small eyes, sunken cheekbones, and bony shoulders poking through his T-shirt. His bare arms were thin along their full length. He looked undernourished, in Scott's opinion.

"Craig Fletcher, we are in the middle of a major investigation, and we believe you are responsible for the supply and distribution of class A and B drugs which have ended up in the hands of minors. Have you anything to say about that?"

"No comment."

"We believe you supplied drugs to Billy Crowther and Dale Walsh, who are part of an ongoing investigation. Is this the case?"

"No comment."

As Scott continued with his questions, each one was met with a no comment response, a common tactic employed by many suspects keen to avoid implicating themselves. Needing to press home the severity of the situation Fletcher found himself in, Scott changed his approach.

"You see, Fletcher. People like you spread pain and misery. I don't care what you and your druggie mates get up to. What upsets me is when the drugs fall into the hands of unsuspecting victims, especially those underage."

Scott paused for a moment as he locked eyes with Fletcher. Fletcher appeared unperturbed, giving Scott a cold stare.

A knock on the door broke the staring match. An officer poked his head into the room and summoned Scott out. Helen paused the recording until Scott returned a few minutes later and settled back into his seat. He smiled smugly at Fletcher, to make sure he clocked it.

"Right, where were we. Oh, yes. We believe you supplied LSD to one or both of the aforementioned individuals, who then in turn supplied them to two girls aged fourteen and fifteen who then took their own lives whilst under the influence of those drugs. A third teen is fighting for her life. Two girls are dead from drugs we believe you supplied."

"No comment."

"What are you doing with a handgun in your car?"

"No comment."

"Suit yourself, Fletcher," Scott said. "You're only making things harder for yourself. You can have a think about it whilst you're back in the cells."

Scott terminated the interview and sent Fletcher to his cell to sweat it out.

39

A nervous energy hummed inside Scott as he stared out the window at the inky black night. With each hour that passed, he'd sensed them moving closer to justice for the girls. Fletcher was the key; he was certain of that. With a bit of time in the cells, he hoped Fletcher would see sense and start squawking like a parrot. Fletcher had been in contact with all the key players they had spoken to in this investigation so far and getting him to talk would blow this case wide open.

Through the window, Scott's reflection stared back at him. He looked tired. His muscles ached. His belly grumbled.

He sat in his chair, pushed it back to an inclined position, and stared at the ceiling.

"Sleeping on the job?" Abby said, as she appeared in his doorway.

"I wish. Only if I could get this to stop working over-time." Scott jabbed a finger into his temple.

"I can stay if you want me to. If you need me?"

Scott offered her a smile. "As much as I would enjoy your company this evening, in the surroundings of this salubrious environment –" Scott laughed, looking around his room, "– your kids need you more. Get yourself home, and I'll see you in the morning."

After Abby left, Scott must have fallen asleep because a voice startled him awake. "Guv... guv."

Scott blinked and yawned loudly. He glanced at the time on his computer. He'd been asleep for nearly half an hour.

Shit.

"What is it?" he said to the officer standing in his doorway. She looked embarrassed and stared at her feet.

"Mike needs to see you. He believes he's found something significant."

The news sent Scott dashing out past the junior officer and onto the main floor, where he found an animated Mike staring at his computer screen and shuffling through stacks of paperwork on his desk.

"Guv, we've been looking at that old fella's CCTV footage. It's a treasure trove. We identified a clip of Duncan picking up several bricks from behind the chip shop and taking them back to his car. It could be something harmless on the face of it and he may have already asked the builders for permission, but he only picked up three bricks."

"That's great work, Mike. I'd like to make Duncan our chief suspect now. We've found drugs on his premises, and he's taken three bricks from the very same pile that had a pattern matching those found in Mia's bag."

"And he's not answering his phone, and no one has seen him for a few days," Mike added.

"Anything else come up in the background search on Duncan Prowse?" Scott shouted to the officers on the CID floor. Various officers poked their heads up from behind their computer screens.

A female officer waved her pen in the air. "Guv, I've been doing a search of Mia's phone records. There was a lot of call traffic between her number and an unregistered number. It's the same one we discovered on Kitty and Claudia's phones. But... there was one call she made to a new number. When I cross-referenced it, it belonged to Duncan."

Scott punched a fist in the air. "Result. I can't see any reason why Mia would have to call Duncan. Mike, get a warrant organised to search his apartment. I want to know what he's hiding."

"What about Fletcher?" Mike asked.

"He can wait. Let's go."

WITH A WARRANT ORGANISED, the commotion and noise of Mike barging his shoulder into Duncan's apartment door led to neighbours peering through doorways, a mixture of concern and curiosity on their faces.

The flimsy door offered little resistance as it succumbed to Mike's large frame, with splinters scattering across the hallway.

Mike split off and started searching rooms on the left, whilst Scott began his search on the right. First impressions suggested the apartment had been used recently. A half carton of milk sat on the kitchen table with an expiry date of the day before; the kitchen bin overflowed; and a dirty breakfast bowl and mug sat in the sink. Scott had called in a drugs dog and retreated out to the hallway with Mike whilst the canine did its job to sweep the apartment.

Scott's initial excitement and anticipation faded when the search for drugs came up empty. He was sure there would be evidence of drugs being used or held on the premises. Frustrated but unperturbed, Scott and Mike continued their search.

Scott sifted through a stack of papers on the lounge table. They were mainly utility bills and circulars. He raised a brow when he stumbled upon a bank statement with dozens of transactions for food deliveries. It appeared Duncan lived on takeaways from Just Eat and Deliveroo.

One thing he did notice as he walked around the apartment was the lack of personal effects. There were no family photographs, or pictures of holidays. In fact, the walls were bare, as if the personal touch and emotions had been stripped from the very fabric of the apartment.

He was torn away from his thoughts when Mike yelled for him.

Mike was crouching beside the bed inside the only bedroom. The mattress had been pulled to one side and was hanging off the edge. "I found these, guv."

Scott flicked through the papers. The first was a logbook transfer document for a red Kia Picanto on a sixty-four plate. The car had been purchased four weeks ago by Duncan.

"Call Helen and get her to run this plate through the ANPR database immediately," Scott said. "Let's check its movements."

"We've got this as well," Mike added, passing Scott further paperwork before pulling out his mobile and calling Helen. It related to a rental agreement on another apartment in Kemptown. The agreement was in Duncan's name. The realisation hit Mike and Scott at the same time. They bagged up the evidence quickly and rushed out of the apartment.

The drive across town took minutes with Mike flooring the accelerator of the job car. He threw it around corners as if competing in the Silverstone Grand Prix. Scott clung to the door handle as he relayed the findings of their search to Helen back at the station. In the short time they had been travelling, Helen had come back with startling information. Mike's request for ANPR data on Duncan's Kia had picked up the car's movements along the seafront on Marine Parade at the exact time Mia had been on the pier. His vehicle had been less than two hundred yards away from her location.

Scott felt his insides turn and his skin prickle. His mouth went dry as another image formed in his mind. He didn't like what he saw.

The second location heightened Scott's concerns. The address was two streets away from where Fletcher had been apprehended. Scott tried every buzzer on the communal door till someone answered and let them in. They charged up the stairs to the second floor before stopping at the apartment. Scott rested his ear on the door, listening for any signs someone was home. Silence greeted him.

Mike hammered on the door. "It's the police. If anyone is in, come to the door now!" he shouted.

An uncomfortable pause followed, and when there was no response, Scott gave Mike the go-ahead to kick the door in. Mike took a few steps back before launching himself forward and planting his foot on the locks. The door shifted but didn't budge. Mike steadied himself and tried again. The door creaked in its frame, the first cracks appearing. On the third occasion the door relented, swinging back and crashing against the walls of the hallway.

Mike burst through first, shouting, "Police! If anyone is here, show yourself now!" He charged down the hallway, as if charging through a rugby pack, casting a glance in each room he passed.

If the last apartment had felt soulless and not lived in unloved, this apartment felt even less so. Scott moved through each of the rooms, looking for signs of recent activity. The place was sparsely decorated with just the bare essentials in each room. Again, there were no signs of life, no trinkets, no framed photographs pinned to the walls or memories standing proudly on shelves for all to see.

Scott moved towards the lounge window. As he did, he stared out at the darkened street. He checked up and down the road for any signs of movement. On a cold January night, with frost in the air, only the bravest ventured out.

He returned to his search. An empty mug with tea stains sat on a small table by an armchair. Biscuit wrappers were scattered around it. He stopped by the alcove and rummaged through a pile of letters placed to one side. Bank statements sat amongst the pile, relating to a different bank account in Duncan's name.

Four weeks ago, Duncan Prowse had purchased a car, opened a second bank account, and taken up tenancy on a second apartment.

"Guv, you've got to see this," Mike said, as he joined Scott in the lounge. He held up several clear evidence bags. "One is definitely weed. The second is a white powder which I reckon is coke, and the third looks familiar. Have a look." He passed one bag to him.

Scott turned over the evidence bag in his hand. A small, clear bag inside contained a quantity of brown tablets. Each one had a picture of a crown imprinted on it. He looked up at Mike, who gave him a knowing nod.

"And that's not all," Mike continued, passing a larger,

clear evidence bag to Scott. It contained a brown scarf. A little white label poked out from one side of the scarf, confirming it was purchased from Miss Selfridge. "I found this tucked at the back of his wardrobe. Souvenir?"

Scott opened the evidence bag and brought the opening closer to his nose. A distinct smell of perfume tickled his senses. "I can't imagine him shopping in Miss Selfridge, can you?"

"What if it belonged to one of the girls?"

"That's a clear possibility, Mike. We'll need to get it to forensics. We can also get one of the team to check with each set of parents to see if one of the girls owned a scarf like this."

Helen called with a further update as Scott and Mike were wrapping up their initial search before calling in SOCO.

"Guv, I've got a traffic camera which picked up a red Kia going through red traffic lights. The plates are a match, and though the image is partially obscured, Duncan is definitely driving... and he has a passenger."

Scott held his breath.

"It's not a very clear image, but the passenger is a smaller female. But I would say she's definitely not an adult."

"We need all available resources to find Duncan Prowse. Alert all units in the Brighton and Hove area to look out for him and alert the rail station to check their security cameras, in case he's already done a runner. Get a picture of him over to them as soon as you can, Helen."

"Yes, guv."

"That's really good work, Helen."

"Thanks, guv."

Scott and Mike retreated from the apartment, not

wishing to contaminate the scene any further before SOCO's arrival. The tenancy agreement confirmed the apartment came with an allocated parking space and a small storage unit beneath the apartment block. They located Duncan's Honda CR-V and called in a recovery truck to remove it for forensic assessment.

They woke the caretaker as a matter of urgency so they could access the storage units beneath the building.

"This bloody better be worth it," the middle-aged man muttered, half asleep as he punched in a digital access code to the door leading to the storage area. The man stood there in his pyjamas and dressing gown, watching Scott and Mike move down the row of doors until they found the correct unit. It had a padlock on it that neither of them had a key to. The annoyed caretaker traipsed off and returned a few minutes later with a crowbar.

Mike wedged one end of the crowbar behind the hasp and used all his weight to pull it back. The metal snapped under the force, sending Mike reeling backwards. He lost his footing and landed flat on his backside.

"You okay, Mike?" Scott asked, hiding a smile that threatened to become a roar of laughter.

Mike rolled over onto his front, getting on his hands and knees to steady himself. "Jesus, my fucking arse hurts."

"You should count yourself lucky you've got enough padding there."

"Ha ha, bloody funny. It's always me that does the grunt work."

"Oh, shut up, Mike. You love getting stuck into the thick of it. You wouldn't have it any other way."

Mike got to his feet, and winced in pain as he grabbed his butt cheeks.

Scott opened the door to the storage unit and squinted. With the absence of any fixed light switch, the small unit was dark and gloomy. Scott pulled out his phone and switched on the torch function, to light up the space.

"What the fuck...?" Mike uttered in confusion.

One small, black case sat in the middle of the floor inside the four- by eight-foot space. Nothing else.

Scott snapped on a pair of latex gloves and flicked open the catches, to reveal a few small newspaper clippings. They were from local newspapers dating back more than twenty years. Each report carried the same picture of a young boy sitting up in hospital, looking miserable and dejected.

The headlines had been sensationalised.

Young schoolboy repeatedly stabbed by playground bullies.

As Scott scanned through each of the articles, the boy's name jumped out at him.

Duncan Prowse.

40

"Why didn't you wake me?" Scott said, still half asleep as he dragged his weary body into the kitchen. He stretched his arms above his head to loosen his stiff shoulders.

"I didn't want to wake you, sweetheart," Cara replied. "You got in so late last night, I thought you should skip your run this morning and have an extra hour in bed." She gave Scott a morning kiss on the cheek. "I made you breakfast. Sit down and I'll bring it over."

Scott blinked furiously and rubbed the sleep from his eyes. He took a seat. "Seriously, you made breakfast?"

Cara came up behind him, and put down a bowl of piping-hot porridge, sprinkled with blueberries, honey, and Chia seeds, as well as a mug of coffee. "Get this down you. I've just popped on toast for you."

Scott pulled Cara into him and wrapped an arm around her waist. "I don't deserve you sometimes. I love how you're so thoughtful and considerate."

"You're always doing things for me, and just knowing I

make your life easier makes me happy," she replied, pulling away to retrieve his toast.

"I'm not sure about making my life easier..." Scott teased.

Cara returned and clipped him around the head for his cheek. She planted a kiss on the top of it and dashed out to work.

Scott spooned large mouthfuls of porridge, savouring the taste and sweetness of the blueberries and honey. It was just what he needed. It had been early morning by the time Scott had arrived home, and he'd barely had five hours of sleep before waking.

His mind switched to the events of last night. Duncan Prowse hadn't figured in their investigations so far, and Scott was kicking himself for focusing too much on the obvious suspects, those who'd had frequent contact with the girls. He had learnt a valuable lesson, that things weren't always as obvious as they seem.

Duncan's motive still bothered Scott. Was he a predator, or a psychologically unbalanced individual with a split personality? When he'd first met Duncan, he hadn't presented himself in a way that had concerned Scott.

Today felt different. He could feel it in his bones. The case was going to go one way or another. SOCO and search officers had been deployed to both apartments overnight, and the results from their searches would be imminent.

Scott's phone buzzed on the kitchen worktop. He tutted before getting up to retrieve it. It was Abby.

"Morning," he answered, putting on his best bright-and-breezy voice.

"You sound chirpy?"

"Yep, just my usual cheerful disposition," Scott replied.

"You? Chirpy? Cheerful? Are you sure we're talking about you?"

"You can go off people very quickly."

Abby laughed. "I've just been catching up with the notes on the system from last night. It looks like you had a good result. That's definite progress."

"We are not there yet."

"Well, I think we are about to move another step closer. A night in the cells seems to have done wonders for Fletcher. He wants to talk."

"I'm on my way," Scott replied hurriedly, as he raced upstairs to throw on clothes.

SCOTT'S physical assessment of Fletcher hadn't changed since the first meeting. If anything, he looked worse. His face appeared gaunt, a lack of sleep no doubt contributing to his haggard features. His clothes were crumpled, and his teeth looked like they were in dire need of a good clean at the dentist.

Abby scrunched up her nose as the man's BO crept across the table and seeped into her nostrils. His bad breath only added to the nausea washing over her.

Scott began by saying, "So, we find ourselves again sitting across the table, waiting for you to do the right thing and open that trap of yours."

Fletcher looked around sheepishly, before tucking his hands under his thighs and pulling his shoulders up towards his ears.

"You told officers you wanted to talk. Well, talk." Scott looked at his watch. "Time is ticking away, and the longer you keep your mouth shut, the deeper you're slipping into trouble. Let me remind you, there's a high probability the drugs you supplied were responsible for the deaths of two young girls. A third is in hospital and may not pull through. You already have to live with that on your conscience, not that I think you have one. You put greed and money before anything else."

A sombre silence settled in the room as Scott and Abby waited for Fletcher to say something. A few minutes passed with nothing said.

Scott tutted and rose from his seat. "It's clear you're wasting our time and using this visit to get out of your cell. We are done here. I've got more important things to do."

Scott shuffled his papers together and began to turn.

"I was at school with Duncan. He was one of my best mates back then," Fletcher blurted out.

Scott turned and placed his papers down on the desk.

"That's more like it," he said. He returned to his seat and prompted Fletcher to continue.

"I supplied the drugs to Duncan, and I also supplied stuff to Billy."

"What did Duncan ask for?" Scott asked, as Abby scribbled away on her notepad.

"He needed something special because he wanted to teach someone a lesson."

Scott's head snapped up. "And that didn't set off warning bells in you?"

Fletcher shook his head. "Business is business. I wasn't really bothered about who he was gonna supply it to. I thought it would be someone else of our age, or maybe younger. Not for one minute did I think it was gonna end up in the hands of teenagers."

"Do you think we were born yesterday?" Scott asked. Anger rocketed through him. He gritted his teeth to stop himself from reaching across the table and grabbing Fletcher by the throat for his arrogance. "What did you give Duncan?"

"I sold him fifteen LSD tabs, fifty quid of weed, twenty quid of charlie."

"And you didn't wonder what he was going to do with fifteen LSD tablets?" Scott asked.

"No. No. I swear I didn't know what he needed them for. If I'd known it was for kids, I wouldn't have supplied them. I've got a kid of my own."

Scott's eyes narrowed, and he glared at Fletcher. "As you said, business is business. You're not bothered who the end-user is. You just want the money."

Fletcher rocked back and forth in his chair. His eyes were heavy with tears. "I'm sorry. I'm sorry. I didn't know."

"Get him out of here!" Scott shouted.

He turned a deaf ear to Fletcher's pathetic pleas as he was dragged along the corridor by officers.

SCOTT WAITED for his call to connect. The person on the other end of the line sounded broken and weary. "Mrs Morris, this is Detective Inspector Scott Baker, I thought I'd give you a quick call to update you on our investigation."

"Inspector, thanks for calling." Ellen Morris's voice sounded flat.

"How are you and your husband holding up?" Scott didn't want to ask, knowing how broken he'd felt at losing his own child, but in a way, he wanted to show he genuinely cared.

"I wish I knew. Sometimes I can sit down and not feel anything. Then there are the times when I feel this over-whelming suffocation and I can't breathe. I can't even bring myself to walk into Kitty's bedroom."

"I know. I wish there was something I could say to make things better. But things are pretty raw at the moment, and it's going to take time to make sense of your loss. But please don't rush it. When I lost my daughter, someone said the same thing to me, and it went in one ear and out the other. How could someone else understand the pain I was going through, or the dark place I had found myself in? And yes, there were times when I thought I would never come out the other side. That's why I am saying give yourself the space to allow every emotion to be experienced. Don't bottle up anything."

Scott could hear Ellen breathing softly on the other end of the line.

"Thank you, Inspector. That means a lot."

"Well, I'm always here if you want to talk to me. I also wanted to let you know we've arrested one individual who we believe was responsible for supplying drugs that Kitty consumed. As far as we know, he didn't directly pass them onto her, and we believe others are involved. We are contin-uing our investigations, and believe we are closing in on another suspect who may have had direct dealings with your daughter, as well as Claudia and Mia."

Ellen gasped. "Who is it?"

"At the moment, I'm not in a position to divulge that information. Not because I don't want you to know, but because it's an active investigation and until I have apprehended everyone and anyone involved in this, I won't be able to release any names. But I promise you, as soon as I am, I will personally come and see you and answer all your questions."

Ellen's voice cracked at the other end. Scott imagined tears flowing down her cheeks.

He finished his call not long after and was determined to live up to that promise. He let out a deep sigh as heaviness sat on his chest. For a brief moment, he looked at the picture of Tina and Becky in happier times. He clenched his fist and took a deep breath before dialling the next number.

He knew the call to Claudia's and Mia's parents would be just as difficult.

***

SCOTT CLEARED his throat and wiped a tear from his eye as he left his office for the CID floor. The team had pulled out all the stops and were chasing down every lead, piece of evidence, and information source available to them.

"Guv," Helen said, thrusting data sheets at him. "This is the ANPR data on Duncan's Honda CR-V. He's not been picked up on any ANPR or traffic cameras over the past week. My guess is the car has been parked up all that time."

"I sense there is a but in your tone, Helen."

"Yes, guv. The nearest ANPR cameras to the school picked up his CR-V on more than nine occasions in the week preceding Kitty's disappearance."

"And nothing after that?" Scott asked.

"Not in that car, guv. I think he then switched to the Kia. It was picked up on traffic and ANPR cameras in the vicinity of the school five times. And we've got residential CCTV footage from a house behind the school perimeter which picks up a red Kia driving past on three occasions, and interestingly, they are all on the days the girls went missing."

"He was picking them up in the Kia?"

"It appears so, guv. Although the footage doesn't confirm who was driving the Kia on those five occasions."

Several other officers fed information into Scott. The investigation was picking up pace. Further sightings of Duncan had been noted on security footage from Palace Pier, two days before Mia was there. Duncan was seen standing in the same spot she'd been found in, peering over the side of the railings at the water below.

"The cell site analysis is looking good," Abby said, interrupting a discussion Scott was having with another officer. "Even though Duncan's phone wasn't used it was on, and showed him in the vicinity of the school on lots of occasions. Based on the analysis and the triangulation data, there is a ninety-five-percent probability that cell sites have triangulated his location to an area behind the school, close to the A27."

"Which is where we found a hole in the fence," Scott added.

"Exactly. The triangulation data also puts him close to Palace Pier on the day Mia was found. I wouldn't be surprised if he was watching her from a distance to make sure she went through with the plan."

Abby confirmed the data that suggested Duncan's phone had been in the vicinity of the viaduct and Elm Grove on the days and times when both Kitty and Claudia died.

"The sick bastard. You're probably right. He was watching."

41

Scott sat facing the whiteboard and cast his eye over the evidence, wondering if he'd missed anything. The pictures of Kitty, Claudia, and Mia stared back at him, their smiling faces reflecting a happier time in their lives. He felt nothing but sorrow for Kitty and Claudia, in particular their parents. Their tragic deaths had rocked two families, a school, and the local community. The repercussions could still be felt around the town as flowers continued to be laid at the school gates and at the girls' homes. Counselling teams had been drafted in to give additional support to the pupils affected by the loss of their friends.

Two days had passed without a single sighting of Duncan Prowse. Stop Out was under surveillance as well as his two apartments, in case he returned. Cell mast data hadn't reported any pings on his phone in over forty-eight hours, so it was likely Prowse had switched it off or discarded it.

Scott blew out his cheeks and tutted. It was as if the trail had gone cold. The team had worked tirelessly for the last two days contacting any known friends, family, and associates, without uncovering any further information or leads. It was as if Duncan Prowse had disappeared off the face of the earth. A rare glimmer of hope had excited the team early yesterday morning when a pile of men's clothes had been found in a heap by the shoreline. Scott wondered whether Prowse had taken his own life, and his body was being swept out to sea. That morning though, the news from the forensics unit had confirmed the clothes were not linked to Duncan Prowse. Hair fibres taken from the pillows and bedding at both apartments hadn't matched those discovered on the clothes.

"You're in early, guv," Helen commented, as she made her way to her desk, with Mike following behind her.

"I know. It feels like I've hardly been home for the last few days. Cara's been really patient, but I know she's getting pissed off with me not being around."

"Yeah, but it's not your fault, guv," Mike replied, dropping his keys and phone on the table with a loud clunk. He made an extraordinary amount of noise as he whipped off his suit jacket, pushed his chair to one side, pulled out desk drawers looking for something, and grumbled to himself, before finally settling down.

"The grace of a ballerina," Helen quipped. She rolled her eyes.

"Says the twisted mind of an eco-warrior. Right back at ya, you hippie loving freak," Mike fired back.

They were joined a few minutes later by Raj and Abby, who breezed in and caught the tail-end of the lighthearted feud.

"Before this descends into a full-scale battle, let's have a quick catch up," Scott remarked, as he swivelled his chair around to face his team. "Who wants to go first?"

"I'll go first," Helen said, throwing a smug smile at Mike, who mouthed "teacher's pet" at her. "Forensic reports on the analysis of all the vehicles seized came in last night. Analysis of the builder's van found no DNA or fibres matching any of the girls. They did find trace elements of marijuana in the footwell of the passenger seat, where Dale used to sit." Helen passed around the analysis report on the vehicle before she continued. "Billy's car had traces of marijuana, and they found a single hair fibre belonging to Kitty. We know quite a few kids sat in his car when they joined him around the back of the shops, so that might explain it. There were no other bodily fluid samples in his car linked to any of the girls. They did discover semen traces on the passenger seat, which were a match for Billy."

Abby scrunched her nose in disgust. "He's been shagging in his car."

Helen made a gagging sound before continuing. She highlighted Fletcher's car had no DNA or fibres matching the girls, although they did find trace evidence of drugs, including a large quantity of marijuana seized from the boot of the car. The team were far more interested with the report on Duncan's Honda CR-V. Hair and clothing fibres matching all three girls were found on the front seat along with rope, and a knife hidden under the driver's seat. Although, they couldn't confirm whether all three girls had actually been inside his vehicle or if the vehicle had been contaminated from clothes Duncan was wearing when he'd been in contact with the girls.

"That's why we need to find his red Picanto. I think that

will unlock a lot more forensic evidence for us," Scott speculated.

Mike had been coordinating the search of both apartments. He stepped in next to confirm hair samples belonging to all three girls had been found at the second apartment. No forensic evidence suggested any sexual activity had taken place between Duncan and any of the girls, which was a relief in Scott's mind.

"And the press releases have so far revealed nothing? No new leads coming in on the phones?" Scott asked, as he looked around his team. A few more officers had arrived and joined the impromptu catch up. His question was met with a sea of shaking heads.

Scott left the team to update Meadows. After, he returned to his office to catch up on paperwork and review the case files, in case he had missed anything. The hours slipped by, and he knew team morale was beginning to wane. They knew who they wanted, but it was like Duncan had slipped off the face of the earth. With such a large town, and an ever-changing tide of university students, it was easy to hide amongst a transient population.

"You fancy a spot of lunch?" Abby asked, as she strode into his office.

"It's usually me asking you. You are never hungry."

"Well, I am today, and I don't ask often, so you don't want to miss out on this rare opportunity of me buying you lunch." Abby laughed.

"You don't have to ask twice," Scott replied, grabbing his jacket and coat. He followed Abby out of the building and to a local sandwich bar.

The heaving bustle of lunchtime trade gave the place a warm and inviting atmosphere. Scott and Abby grabbed a table and ordered food. They both enjoyed their coffee whilst their lunch order was being prepared.

Unusually, there were a lot of student types. This wasn't the type of place they normally hung out at, but it soon became clear why. On the blackboard behind the counter, Scott saw that students were entitled to twenty-five per cent off their meals if they had an NUS card. It reminded him of his old university days, The National Union of Students card had given him so many benefits and discounts. Back then, he'd been entitled to a council grant to cover most of his education and living expenses. Nowadays, he wondered how students coped with the excessive student loans.

"It's been a tough case, hasn't it?" Abby said, sipping on her coffee. She savoured it as the liquid trickled down her throat and warmed her belly.

"It has." Scott nodded. "At least we know what we're dealing with now. I spoke to the Conquest Hospital in Hastings yesterday. That was where the pictures of Duncan propped up in a bed had been taken. Apparently, at the time, the news had created quite a stir. His injuries weren't significant, just minor stab wounds. But he was badly roughed up."

"Yep, from what I could see, the newspapers loved it."

Scott wrapped a serviette round his finger whilst he mulled over the insights about Duncan's life. "The school feedback wasn't much better. Duncan was a lonely boy who had found it hard to make friends. From what I could gather, he was the kind of kid who always attracted the wrong attention. He was thin-framed, so often picked on, and his ears stuck out, which meant they often got flicked." Scott thought back to his own childhood. "I remember that happening during my school years. One kid had sticky-out ears. Can't remember his name. But he had them flicked and pulled so often, one of his ears tore at the back."

Abby winced. "That's bloody assault."

"It is. But at the time, I don't think schools took it seriously. If it happened now, you would have a riot on your hands. The parents would be turning up at school. The headmaster fed back to one of our officers that after a particular bout of extended bullying, Duncan turned to food and became overweight, which only led to more bullying. It was a bloody vicious circle." Scott paused when the waitress arrived with their food. He refused the offer of any condiments. After the waitress left, Scott continued. "Other schoolboys pulled his shorts and pants down in PE. The girls in his class ribbed Duncan as a result, and he was singled out by bullies. The final straw was when he was stabbed by a couple of bullies who turned out to be girls."

"Doesn't it make you wonder why kids can be so nasty?" Abby said, picking up her sandwich and then taking a bite.

"Yes, but bullying has always been around, only the methods of bullying have changed. Once upon a time it was all verbal and physical. Now, so much of it is cyber."

They continued to discuss it whilst they satisfied their hunger. Scott was about to order another coffee when his phone rang. He glanced at the screen to see Mike's name pop up on his caller ID.

"Mike, what's up?"

"Guv, there's been a serious disturbance at the Royal Sussex. There was an attempted attack on Mia."

42

Scott slammed on the brakes, his tyres screeching across the tarmac, as his car came to a stop outside the Royal Sussex hospital. Abby was already exiting the car before Scott had pulled his keys out of the ignition. A swarm of uniformed officers were gathered outside the main entrance, usual after a major incident had been declared. An NPAS helicopter had been scrambled from its base and would be arriving shortly.

Mike was already on the scene, liaising with the ground commander and directing officers to do a systematic sweep of the buildings.

Scott and Abby raced over to him and a small huddle of senior officers.

"Mike, what's the current state of play?" he asked.

"There was an attempted attack on Mia less than thirty minutes ago. A man wielding a hammer raced into the paediatric unit and made his way towards Mia's room. Nurses intervened, and Mia's dad stepped out into the hallway when he heard the commotion."

"Any casualties?"

"Nothing serious, guv. A nurse was injured when she tackled the assailant. She hit the floor after receiving an elbow to the face. Mia's dad received a hammer blow to his shoulder. It's mainly bruising, but he's undergoing an X-ray to be safe."

"Abby, can you go and check on Mia?" Scott asked. Abby dashed through the front doors of the hospital seconds later. "Mike, have we got a description?" Scott surveyed the scene.

"The description was a bit vague, but cameras positioned at the entrance to the paediatric ward confirmed it's our man. Duncan Prowse."

Scott turned when he heard the roar of an engine behind him. A BMW X5 armed response vehicle was racing towards the main entrance. The scene was becoming chaotic, as more officers in vans arrived to swell the numbers already searching the hospital.

"Have we got any idea on his location?" Scott enquired as he and Mike made their way into the main reception of the hospital. Members of the public waiting to be seen for their appointments had been ushered out of the building for their own safety. A deathly silence hung in the cavernous space. Reception staff had also been evacuated, allowing police canines and their handlers to start searching the corridors.

"Yes, guv. Cameras tracked him heading down the stairs, away from the paediatric unit, and towards the rear exit. He was then seen crossing a path and heading into the outpatients building. Security cameras lost him for a brief moment, and then picked him up again, crashing through a fire exit, with two hospital security staff giving chase. They lost him when he doubled back and disappeared around the back of storerooms. We've been unable to locate him since."

With such a large area to cover, which included a multi-storey car park, dozens of entry and exit points, and a sprawling estate, which extended to open grounds beyond the hospital, the task they faced was enormous. The priority was to contain the area as best as possible, and Scott was confident uniformed officers, under the instruction of the ground commander, had much of that covered.

He joined a team of officers as they began to search the corridors. Mike splintered off to join a second team as Scott's team weaved through the warren of passageways.

At one point, Scott lost his sense of direction, and paused in the corridor to get his bearings. With each passing minute, the chances of finding Prowse diminished. He'd been receiving updates over the airway that NPAS were circling above the hospital, looking for any signs of movement. It gave Scott reassurance to know that, if Duncan made a run for it, he could be tracked by air.

His radio burst into life. "He's been spotted. The suspect has been seen running through accident and emergency. All units, make your way to that location."

Scott looked up at the hospital signs hanging from the ceiling. He was standing by ENT; Duncan's location was at the other end of the estate.

He raced down the corridor, looking for new signs to steer him in the right direction. He could hear the other officers racing up behind him, the sound of their footsteps bouncing off the walls.

"Mike, where are you?" Scott shouted into his radio.

"Thirty seconds away, guv," responded a breathless Mike.

As Scott burst through the doors of accident and emergency, he was met with utter chaos. Patients waiting to be seen in reception scattered in all directions; chairs were upended and cast to one side as people fled. Reception and nursing staff stood horrified behind a reception counter, protected by a plastic, shatterproof screen.

Scott followed the noise through the doors beyond A&E and into the urgent care centre, where the space opened up into a large reception area, with green chairs fixed in rows to the floor. Towards the far end he saw a scrum of officers, many of whom were shouting and screaming at the tops of their voices.

Mike burst through a different door and didn't hesitate for a moment as he charged towards a pack and threw his weight into the bundle of bodies. Scott saw one officer being dragged away, a large gash on his head leaking blood.

Anger coursed through his veins. Scott stepped in closer. Officers peeled off once the suspect had been detained and secured. A battered and bloodied, Duncan Prowse lay face down on the floor, his hands cuffed behind his back, his ankles strapped together, his face bruised and swollen.

Gasping for breath, his heart threatening to rip from his chest, and his eyes fixed wide, Scott quickly marched to the nearest door and into fresh air.

He bent over, chest heaving, and rested his hands on his knees. His hands tingled as a spike of adrenaline shook his body. His reaction was out of character for him, which only surprised him further.

HAVING BEEN ASSESSED by the police doctor and deemed fit enough for interview, Duncan Prowse sat with a duty solicitor, his hands still cuffed. His face bore the scars of war, with a black eye, a fat bottom lip, and various scratches and grazes.

Scott and Abby stood inside an adjoining room to the interview suite and watched Prowse on the monitor.

Abby's phone pinged with a message. She read it before relaying its contents. "Uniform found a red Kia Picanto abandoned in a prohibited parking area within hospital grounds not long after Prowse was nicked. It's been towed away for forensic analysis."

"That's exactly what we need to nail this bastard," Scott hissed, as he glared at the monitor.

"Are you ready for this?" Abby asked.

"I hope so. The minute I saw Prowse lying on the floor, a picture of Kitty's remains flashed into my mind. Remembering her disfigured body again overwhelmed me. I wanted to go over there and kick the fucking shit out of him. I had to go outside to get a grip."

"Are you okay now?" Abby asked. She placed a hand on his arm, a look of concern softening her face.

Taking a deep breath in and out, he replied, "We are about to find out."

Scott waited for Abby to do the usual formalities, which gave him an opportunity to study Prowse once again. He continued to stare at the table, not wanting to acknowledge Scott's presence.

"Duncan Prowse, we've arrested you on suspicion of being involved in the supply of drugs, abduction, and the deaths of Kitty Morris and Claudia White. You've also been arrested on the supply of drugs, abduction, coercion, and attempted murder of Mia Boswell. You've also been arrested for the assault on two emergency workers, and ABH of Mia's father, Raphael Boswell. Do you understand those charges?" Scott said.

"Yes," Prowse replied, still unwilling to look up.

"We believe you supplied drugs to all three girls, so would you care to explain why?"

Prowse shrugged. "They deserved it. They were bullies. They needed a taste of their own medicine."

"How d'you know they were bullies?" Scott probed.

Prowse stared at the ceiling and let out a long sigh. "Because I saw them picking on someone. I saw them trying to stab a kid a few weeks ago. They were being goaded into stabbing someone while this whole crowd of kids gathered around them, baying for blood."

"Why would that matter so much to you?"

Prowse opened his mouth to speak but then stopped. He looked Scott in the eyes before continuing. "Because I hate bullies."

Scott opened a Manila folder and pulled out press clippings of Duncan as a young boy. He turned the clippings around so Duncan could see them. "Because of this?"

"Yeah. It took me years of counselling and therapy to get over my childhood. I was attacked with a compass and a penknife. I thought I'd finally buried those memories, and all I had left were physical scars as reminders."

"But?" Scott prompted Prowse to continue.

"The day I saw the attack, I had a flashback out of nowhere that unlocked a box in my mind. The feelings of inadequacy, fear, and anger flooded back."

"Anger?" Scott asked.

Prowse nodded. "Yes! *Anger.* Anger because people can get away with things like this. Anger there is no one there to protect you or stand up for you. Anger that you have to fight your battles and your demons alone."

Prowse's hands began to tighten into fists as memories from the past clearly came back to haunt him.

"You could have stopped it and broken up the fight. That would have been the end of it," Abby said.

Prowse shook his head violently. "It never stops. It might have stopped that time, but it would have carried on. Some other time, some other place. If it wasn't that poor kid it would have been another. These bullies never stop once they start. They needed to be stopped. Kitty and Claudia needed to be stopped."

"If it was only Kitty and Claudia, then why did you target Mia?" Scott asked, seeking clarity.

"Because she was there too," Prowse hissed. "She stood there. She didn't take part but she stood and watched. Mia could have stopped it but she didn't. She was as bad as them. My plan for Mia didn't go as well, so I needed to go back and finish her off."

"So how are Billy and Dale connected to all of this?"

Prowse went on to talk about how the girls had been infatuated with Billy. And supplying drugs to Billy through Fletcher had been a way for him to deflect attention away from himself. Leaving drugs under the till was something he was particularly proud of, because it meant making Billy the prime suspect.

"You groomed the girls?" Scott asked.

Prowse shrugged. "I guess. But not in a sexual way. They all fancied Billy and were desperate to get his attention. I said Billy loved girls who acted grownup. And a sure-fire way of getting into his good books was if they dabbled in drugs, because he did."

"And the money and necklaces?"

"Just my way of gaining their trust. I told them Billy asked me to pass those gifts on, because he liked them. And they believed me. They genuinely believed Billy was keen on each of them. Kitty didn't know Claudia fancied Billy, and Claudia didn't know Kitty fancied Billy. That's the way I wanted it. I wanted them to think they were special, and so would go to any lengths to keep it secret."

"And Dale? What part did he play in this twisted game of yours?" Scott asked through gritted teeth.

"Dale was a bonus. They loved him too. It allowed me to make the girls think two older guys were interested in them. And those pricks lapped up the attention."

"And where did you get your drugs from?" Scott knew the answer but needed to hear it, for the benefit of the interview.

"I got them from an old school friend. Craig Fletcher. I told him to pop into the shop and approach Billy about selling weed and gas. And in return, Billy would get a share of the profits and supply to whomever he wanted. Billy, being a greedy fucker, snapped up the opportunity. I supplied Dale because I knew he was big on the club scene." Prowse allowed himself a small smile. "They did my work for me."

"Why did Mia call you? Your phone records show she called your number on one particular occasion."

"Stupid cow. I gave her my number once after she got really pissed off and upset about something. I can't remember what. She turned up at the shop, hoping Billy would cheer her up. But he wasn't there so I consoled her, gave her my number and said that if she was ever upset again, then to call me. I never thought she would. As soon as I got the call, I knew I had to take care of her quickly."

Scott leant back in his chair. "I'm curious. How did you manage to get the girls to come with you?"

"That was easy. I'd already developed a good relationship with all of them. When I called them to tell them Billy was desperate to see them, and he had sent me to pick them up, because he couldn't leave the shop, they willingly came along. I gave each of them chocolate and drinks. Little did they know I'd popped LSD tablets into each drink. They were off their faces within half an hour. It was easy to take them back to my apartment and keep them there. Each time the LSD started to wear off, I'd get them to drink more. By the time I let them go they were so off their faces. It was only going to end one way."

Scott hammered out every last detail with Duncan Prowse before terminating the interview and confirming the charges with Meadows.

43

W hen Scott walked back into CID, the team erupted into cheers. News had already reached them of Prowse's full confession. Scott saw from their faces how good it felt for everyone to strive for something so real, so important. All the long hours, all those gruelling sessions poring over countless hours of CCTV footage had finally counted for something.

But he'd done it. They had done it. And it meant more than a result for them. Every officer bellowed to let him know how much it meant. With the cheers came fists in the air, as the team congratulated one another.

It was all quiet one second when he'd walked in, and then deafening the next, rising to a crescendo and then falling to little more than a trickle before the same triumphant excitement commanded silence once more.

Scott waved his arms in the air. "Settle down, settle down, you lot." He waited for the din of conversations to die down before he continued. "We've got a result, and I want to thank each one of you for your diligence, hard work, and pure dedication in getting this end result. Many of you have put family lives on hold, have let down your partners, and missed reading a bedtime story to your kids. We couldn't have got there without each and every one of you. And you should all be bloody proud of what you've done, because I am. The toerag who was responsible for the deaths of Kitty Morris and Claudia White won't be harming anyone else."

His sentiment was met with nods from the officers perched around him.

"Before we can get down to the pub and start celebrating, and by the way, Abby said she is buying the first round," – Scott didn't risk looking in Abby's direction, knowing she'd be glaring at him at this very moment – "we've still got a lot of work to do. Our job has just started. We've got to make sure we have every single piece of evidence sewn up and in the file, ready for CPS." Scott dismissed his team and told them to get back to work.

Helen nabbed Scott as he was about to head back to his office.

"Guv, I asked the high-tech unit to do their magic and enhance the traffic camera footage of Prowse and his passenger. It's not perfect, but what do you think?" she said, handing him still images.

Scott narrowed his eyes as he focused on the first image. It was still grainy and pixellated but much clearer than the first images he'd seen. It was another damning piece of evidence. Even from the elevated angle of the camera, the outline of his passenger was much clearer. It was Mia. "That's good. That's really good."

"It gets better, guv. SOCO have begun their examination of Duncan's Kia. It will probably take a while, and I doubt we'll get any decent forensic evidence for a day or two, but they discovered a grey Superdry rucksack in the boot. It had Claudia's schoolbooks in it."

"He's practically hanging himself. He was either careless or didn't have time to discard her rucksack before we caught him. Were there any mobile phones in the car?"

"No, guv."

"Okay, pity. That would have been the icing on the cake. The chances are he used a burner phone, and that's probably sitting in a bin somewhere. Good work again, Helen."

Scott left the team to pull all the individual threads of their investigation together into one cohesive framework of evidence that would ensure Duncan Prowse's court case would end with only one outcome.

A lengthy sentence.

44

S cott exchanged an uncomfortable glance with Abby as they stood on the doorstep. He pressed the door-bell and waited. The sound of slow, shuffling foot-steps grew louder beyond the door. A key was turned in the lock, and a tired-looking face appeared.

"Mrs Morris, may we come in?"

Ellen stood back, surprised by the number of visitors at her door.

This was the second visit of the day for Scott, having already visited Claudia's parents to deliver the same news. Claudia's parents had been grief-stricken, and the visit had been painful. The scarf discovered at Duncan's second apart-ment had belonged to Claudia. Hair fibres retrieved through forensic analysis were a match to Claudia and Duncan. Claudia's parents had wanted the scarf back. Scott had refused but promised that once sentencing was over, Clau-dia's possessions would be returned to them.

Scott had asked Claudia's parents to accompany them to

the Morris household for a particular reason, and they'd willingly agreed to come along.

Ellen nodded weakly as she stepped aside and showed all four of them into the lounge.

Alan Morris sat slumped in an armchair, clinging to a T-shirt. He glanced up and offered them a slight smile. He had the face of a broken man. Unshaven for days, dark circles around his eyes, and bloodshot eyes, he looked like a man who had travelled to hell and back again. He held out a limp hand and shook Frank's extended one.

Alan Morris noticed Scott staring at the T-shirt. "Kitty's favourite top. It was sitting on the floor. It smells of her – that unique smell only your own child has. It still feels like she's here." His eyes watered again and his chin wobbled.

Scott and Abby took a seat opposite him. Ellen joined her husband and sat on one of the armrests beside him. The Whites sat on one end of the sofa; Emma's hand was cocooned in her husband's large mitts.

A few seconds of silence passed with neither side knowing what to say. Scott noticed Abby was visibly moved as she stared straight ahead, her eyes wide, and clutching the edges of her coat.

"I promised I would come and see you as soon as we had news. We've charged a second suspect in connection with your daughter's death. We have enough evidence to confirm he was responsible for supplying drugs to Kitty. I know it's not any consolation, but I wanted you to know everyone involved in your daughter's death will face the full force of the law."

"Who was he?" Ellen asked, her voice barely audible.

"He was a shopkeeper. Owned a place where kids would hang out after school. He targeted three individuals, including Kitty. I'm sorry we couldn't get to Kitty sooner," Scott said, bowing his head for a moment.

Ellen cleared her throat and wiped her nose with a tissue. "It's not your fault. You've done everything asked of you. The person who took our little girl has been caught. Let's hope he can't harm anyone else."

"We'll be pushing for the maximum sentences available under the law. There is enough evidence to make sure he won't get out for a very, very long time."

"Why our Kitty? Why did he choose her?"

Scott couldn't tell her the truth. Not yet. The emotions were still raw. How could he tell Alan and Ellen Morris their daughter was a bully, and that she'd been punished for being one? There weren't many parents who could accept such an accusation. "We are not a hundred percent sure. The suspect will be undergoing psychiatric evaluation, and at the moment I don't think it's something we should be talking about. The main point is we've found the person responsible for Kitty's death, and I hope it helps you come to terms with your loss."

The Morrises nodded, exchanging supportive looks between one another.

"Is there anything else we can help you with at the moment? I know how difficult this is for you."

"I know, Inspector," Ellen replied. "You've experienced grief in much the same way we have. Knowing you understand our pain reassures us you have our best interests at heart." Tears rolled down her cheeks; her shoulders heaved, and a screech of a cry tore from her throat. She threw a hand over her mouth. "I don't know how we can continue. Kitty... Kitty... was our life. She brought us fun, laughter, stress, headaches, but she made our lives complete. Isn't that what being a parent is all about?"

"It is, Ellen. That's why I asked Emma and Frank to come with us today. Emma, you wanted to say something…" Scott prompted, as he turned to look at her.

Emma sniffed as she grabbed a tissue from her pocket. She dabbed her red, swollen eyes. "I guess we're feeling the same pain. We've both lost our daughters, and nothing will bring them back, but perhaps talking about it together might help us all get through this."

Ellen offered the smallest of smiles as she rested her head on her husband's shoulder. When the words wouldn't come the tears did instead.

"I'm sure you could all find comfort in the support. I know when I lost my family, having others around me helped me through the darkest days," Scott said, looking across to Abby who gritted her teeth. She blinked hard to fight away the tears as her gaze flicked from the parents to Scott and back.

Frank remained tight-lipped as his chest heaved. He held his wife's hand tight, almost too tight on occasion, as rage clearly still coursed through his veins. The grief surged out with every expelled breath, always reaching higher peaks and never sufficiently soothed by his long intakes of air.

Scott felt the weight of their personal agony. The power of such profound grief felt like emptiness in your heart, a sheer nothingness that somehow took over and held your soul hostage as it threatened to kill you entirely. God, he'd been there countless times not long after losing his family. It was a heavy feeling, like the weight of the world was resting on his shoulders, and there was nothing he could do to get out from under it.

"Does it ever get any easier, Inspector?" Alan whispered, his fingers wrapped tight around Kitty's top. His eyes were swollen, with dark circles and bulging lower lids.

Scott bowed his head for a moment, deciding on the most sensitive words. "Yes. At the time I was so confused and broken that it was hard for me to see a way forward. But things do settle down – with time. The pain fades, the good memories remain, and you realise that life has to go on."

Ellen stood and walked over to Emma who got up to meet her. They stared at each another for a few seconds before embracing in a hug. It created a sense of stillness in the room for a few moments.

Scott blew out his cheeks as he looked at Abby. She was sitting with her hands clenched and buried deep in her lap.

Alan summoned the courage to make the first move by rising from his seat and walking slowly over to Frank.

Frank stared at the floor, lost in his thoughts.

"Frank..." Alan said.

The man cleared his throat and rose, his eyes shifting in every direction. He slowly extended a hand, which Alan took, before pulling him in for a hug. They consoled one another.

Scott offered a sympathetic nod and left his card with them. Ellen showed them out.

As he and Abby stood on the pavement by his car, Scott took a deep breath and let out a long sigh. Abby wiped away tears that streaked her face. The visit had affected them both deeply.

"You going to be okay?" he asked.

Abby couldn't reply. A lump of sadness had stuck in her throat. Her eyes welled up as she bit her bottom lip.

Scott reached out and gave her a hug. "That's the shit part of our job."

Abby nodded. "And it never gets any easier," came her muffled reply. She peeled herself away from Scott. "Look at the state of me. I probably look like a freak from a Halloween horror night movie."

She used the back of her sleeve to wipe her teary eyes and red, runny nose.

Scott tilted his head to one side and examined Abby for a moment. "Now that you mention it..."

Abby swung a playful punch at Scott, connecting with his arm. "There's more of that, you git."

"Oi, that's assaulting a senior officer. I could have you demoted for that."

"Yeah, yeah. Promises, promises!" Abby shouted, walking around to the passenger side. She narrowed her eyes and smiled.

"What's that look for?" Scott asked, unlocking the car.

"Thanks. That's all I'll say."

And that's all she needed to say. Scott knew it was Abby's way of saying thank you for supporting her a few moments ago, like a true friend.

As Scott put his keys in the ignition, his phone rang. He unzipped his coat and patted down his jacket to locate his phone. He pulled it out to see Mike's number on the screen.

"Mike, we're on our way back."

"Great. I thought I'd let you know I've received a call from the hospital. It's Mia."

Scott felt a tightening in his chest, as a veil of dread smothered him. He put his phone on loudspeaker and stared at Abby, dreading the next few words.

"She's woken up, guv."

The words slipped through Scott's awareness as he stared at Abby.

"Guv, did you hear me? Mia has woken up, and the first thing she said was 'Mum,' and squeezed her mum's hand. How bloody good is that?"

Scott snapped out of his daze when he noticed the euphoria in Mike's voice. "That's brilliant. Absolutely bloody brilliant."

Abby grinned and pumped her fist.

Scott hung up, speechless for once. The pair sat in silence for a few minutes, the pain, stress, and adrenaline seeping from their bodies, leaving them exhausted.

"Shall we get something to eat? I'm hungry," Scott asked, turning to Abby.

"I thought you'd never ask. Your shout."

WE HOPE YOU ENJOYED THIS BOOK

If you could spend a moment to write an honest review on Amazon, no matter how short, we would be extremely grateful. They really do help readers discover new authors.

ALSO BY JAY NADAL

TIME TO DIE

(Book 1 in the DI Scott Baker series)

THE STOLEN GIRLS

(Book 2 in the DI Scott Baker series)

ONE DEADLY LESSON

(Book 3 in the DI Scott Baker series)

IN PLAIN SIGHT

(Book 4 in the DI Scott Baker series)

AN EVIL OFFERING

(Book 5 in the DI Scott Baker series)

EYE FOR AN EYE

(Book 6 in the DI Scott Baker series)

MARKED FOR DEATH

(Book 7 in the DI Scott Baker series)

DIE FOR ME

(Book 8 in the DI Scott Baker series)

Printed in Great Britain
by Amazon

28247112R00153